He was going to kiss her

She could see the longing in his eyes.

His lips touched hers softly. They opened. She followed suit, and his tongue pushed through.

His hands caressed her smooth back and she pressed her fingers into his taut shoulder muscles, desperate to get closer. He lifted her, holding her naked body flush against his own in the flowing river.

She placed her arms around his neck and let her legs encircle his hips. The roar of the river pounded in her ears.

He left her mouth and she whimpered in disappointment. But then he kissed her neck, slipped his hands lower to cup her bottom, and she tightened her knees against him.

"Robin?" His strangled voice was filled with need.

"Yes, Jake?"

"You don't want this."

"What?" She wanted this more than she'd ever wanted anything in her life. She was his for the taking.

When he spoke again was precise. "You're R Jacob Bronson. And y to happen."

D0816146

Dear Reader,

People accuse me of being too decisive. Okay, I'll be honest, they accuse me of being too impulsive. I plan as little as possible, because there's nothing more frustrating than strategizing and formulating for days, weeks, or years on end when you could spend that time actually *doing* something. In *Forever Jake*, I wanted to feature an impulsive heroine, someone who has an idea and immediately springs into action.

When Robin Medford decides she wants to have a baby, she doesn't waste time wandering willy-nilly around the notion. And when she decides Jacob Bronson is the perfect candidate to father her baby, she immediately springs into action, all right—with unexpected results!

I hope you enjoy *Forever Jake*. Temptation has long been my favorite of the Harlequin lines, and I am absolutely thrilled to be in such talented company.

Best wishes,

Barbara Dunlop

Books by Barbara Dunlop

HARLEQUIN DUETS
54B—THE MOUNTIE STEALS A WIFE

FOREVER JAKE
Barbara Dunlop

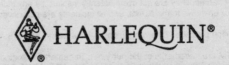

HARLEQUIN®

TORONTO • NEW YORK • LONDON
AMSTERDAM • PARIS • SYDNEY • HAMBURG
STOCKHOLM • ATHENS • TOKYO • MILAN • MADRID
PRAGUE • WARSAW • BUDAPEST • AUCKLAND

For Marcelle Dubé.
With admiration, respect and gratitude.

ISBN 0-373-25948-4

FOREVER JAKE

Copyright © 2001 by Barbara Dunlop.

This edition published by arrangement with Harlequin Books S.A.

Visit us at www.eHarlequin.com

Printed in U.S.A.

1

A WOMAN simply couldn't trust sperm banks these days.

Robin Medford stuffed the latest copy of *The New England Journal of Medicine* into the leather backpack tucked beneath the airplane seat in front of her. The Beaver floatplane shuddered as it banked left, bringing the town of Forever into view through the tiny oblong window.

Following a long-standing custom in the remote Yukon Territory, the pilot buzzed the small town nestled between a steep, sparsely treed mountainside and the lazy winding blue-green river that was its namesake. Then he swooped over the town hall to determine wind direction by the Canadian and Yukon flags flapping out front in the sunny afternoon breeze.

Taking a deep breath, Robin turned away from the window and let her head fall back against the high-backed seat. It amazed her to read how many mistakes were made by well-meaning fertility doctors and laboratory technicians. Some of the results were downright frightening.

It had taken less than three days' research to convince her that sperm banks were not a reliable source for her future child's genetic start in life. Which narrowed her options somewhat, but didn't necessarily cancel her plan.

She'd simply have to get pregnant the old-fashioned way. Find a promising specimen, pick a fertile day, and send in the troops. Piece of cake, really.

After all, she reasoned, she'd had sex with Juan Carlos at the base camp below Mount Edelrich in Switzerland two years ago. It certainly wasn't rocket science. In fact, her final paramedic qualification exam had been a whole lot more complicated than Juan—and a whole lot more exciting as she recalled.

She could do it again to get a baby. Not with Juan, of course. Aside from being half a world away, he was far too narcissistic and self-indulgent to be a candidate for fatherhood.

The pilot banked the plane more steeply, coming about above a poplar grove and into the wind as he lined up with the river on his final approach. Robin imagined the stick under her fingertips and automatically checked out the window for debris in the high-running, late August river.

As the water rushed up to meet them, she pictured adjustments to the flaps and watched the altimeter in her mind's eye. It had been a long time since she'd piloted a Beaver—longer still since she'd visited the small town where she'd grown up.

Fifteen years to be exact.

Fifteen years since she'd graduated from high school and set off to find adventure. She'd been determined to build a life beyond the isolated community that lay three hundred miles north of the Alaska Highway, up against the border of the Northwest Territories.

She'd succeeded.

The Beaver's floats sliced through the river current. The force of deceleration pinned her against her seat belt as the craft succumbed to the resistance of the water. The pilot backed off the prop speed, and she settled back into her seat.

She'd succeeded, both in building herself a career and in seeing a good portion of the world. And now she'd come full circle. For the first time, she was back home. She removed the hard plastic ear muffs that protected her hearing against the loud radial engine. Then she ran spread fingers through her long, wavy hair as they chugged toward the gray dock.

Forever. A town founded by miners, then kept alive by wilderness tourism and the manufacture of fine furniture from the rare russet birch trees that graced the nearby mountains. The streets were still dusty, the buildings still weathered, and the surrounding wilderness still dwarfed the efforts of nine hundred and fifty townspeople.

The floats groaned against the tire bumpers on the dock as the plane came to a halt. Robin flipped her seat belt catch. When the door swung open, she auto-

matically steeled herself against the impending on-
slaught of mosquitoes and blackflies.

Biting insects notwithstanding, she was surpris-
ingly glad to be back. She could hardly wait to see the
expression on her grandmother's face when she realized that every single one of her children, grandchildren and great-grandchildren was here to celebrate
her seventy-fifth birthday.

Robin had five days to spend with her family before she had to report to her new job at Wild Ones
Tours in Toronto. It was good to arrive, but she was
certain she'd be more than ready to get back to civili-
zation by the time her five days were up.

Even now, Forever was extremely isolated. There
was no road access to the town and no airport. People
came and went by boat and floatplane or they didn't
come and go at all.

Besides, she was a woman with an all new fertility
plan. She needed to get back to where there were
men. Real men. Intelligent, genetically sound men
who liked sex.

She sized up the pilot as he helped her across the
airplane float and onto the swaying dock. He was a
bit too short. She smiled her thanks and swung the
backpack onto her shoulders.

This whole sperm bank risk factor could end up
working in her favor. Upon reflection, it definitely
made sense to meet and get to know the biological father of her planned child. A woman could learn a
whole lot more about a person through conversation

and observation than through a sterile file in a clinic waiting room.

She placed her palm against her abdomen and smiled as the soles of her leather boots crunched on the gravel of River Front Road. According to her fertility books, at thirty-two she was still within an age group highly ranked for safe conception and delivery. She had secured an excellent promotion that would keep her in a beautiful city. And she had her name on the waiting list of the best nanny agencies and preschools available.

Everything was in place. All she needed was the right man for about twenty minutes.

JAKE BRONSON HEARD the Beaver's engine slow to a stop from his narrow hiding place between the Fireweed Café and the Forever Hardware Store. He pulled his battered Stetson hat low on his forehead and leaned back, trying to fade into the raw wood siding of the café wall.

He wasn't normally a coward, but ever since his former friend Derek Sullivan had placed that ridiculous personal ad in newspapers all across the county, the women of Forever had declared open season on Jake. Oh, not that they really wanted to marry him. At least, he didn't *think* they really wanted to marry him.

He was pretty sure all three of the very public marriage proposals last week were jokes. But Annie Miller was heading down Main Street right now, and she looked frighteningly purposeful to a jaded Jake. She wore a sundress far too pretty for an ordinary Saturday afternoon.

Jake had no intention of being the butt of yet another public prank.

He stood stock-still, watching Annie from the corner of his eye, breathing carefully. A long, low growl sounded beside him. He cringed, knowing exactly what was coming next.

A series of deep-chested barks echoed through the narrow passageway, nearly deafening him and seriously compromising his attempt at secrecy. His heart sank as he turned to face the huge husky-wolf cross who had ferreted him out and was standing, hackles raised, about three feet away.

Dweedle-Dumb was a darn sight more impressive than his name suggested. He ruled the streets of Forever with an iron paw, sending lesser animals scurrying out of his way with a sidelong glance and a curled lip. Jake briefly considered trying to shush the animal, but knew from experience that Dweedle-Dumb's owner, the town farrier, was the only person who had any influence.

"Dweedle, hi-yup." The harsh command was music to Jake's ears.

"What the hell are you doing hanging out in the shadows, Jake?" Patrick Moore ambled to the spot where Dweedle-Dumb now sat obediently in the center of the dirt path, all traces of cunning in his yellow eyes replaced by adoration for his master.

Jake placed a finger across his lips in a silent signal,

jerking his head sideways toward Annie. She was fifty yards away and closing.

Patrick squinted out into the street. Then his ruddy face broke into a grin and his body shook with suppressed mirth. To his credit, he didn't make a sound. Although Jake was having a hard time being grateful for that tender mercy.

"Looks a bit dressed up there, doesn't she?" Patrick whispered.

"That's what worries me," said Jake.

"Heard she made moss-berry squares this morning. Do you suppose she'll try to impress you with her culinary expertise?"

"She doesn't want to impress me. She wants to embarrass me." Jake ducked his head, hoping the hat brim would hide any telltale flash of his face.

"She's turning," Patrick announced.

"Toward us?" Jake didn't dare look up.

"No. To the dock. Whoa, mama."

"What?"

"Now that's a sweet sight."

"What is it?" Jake hissed, braving a brief glance out onto the street.

"Wouldn't mind having *her* answer my personal ad." Patrick straightened his shoulders and tucked his plaid shirt into the waistband of his jeans.

"You don't have a personal ad." The lucky man.

As Jake's vision adjusted to the bright sunshine, he felt a jolt course directly through his nervous system. A tall, willowy blonde greeted Annie with an exuberant hug right there in front of the northern pike fountain. She was wearing formfitting jeans and a brightly colored cardigan sweater. The sweater was open, revealing a white knit shirt.

Even from thirty yards away Jake was struck by the beauty of her profile. Her sandy hair glinted in the sunshine and her tinkling laughter seemed to brighten the dusty street. For a second he actually hoped she *had* answered the ad.

That was ridiculous, of course. Because Derek's ad didn't say where Jake lived. The chances of some big-city bombshell figuring out that "Yukon Jake" lived in Forever were somewhere well south of nil.

Patrick raked his hair back off his forehead. "Didn't know Annie had friends that looked like that."

"Going over to meet her?" asked Jake. He slouched against the wall, hooking his thumbs into his belt loops and crossing one dusty cowboy boot over the other. He let his gaze slide appreciatively over her shapely thighs and cute derriere.

"Reckon I might just do that." Patrick squared his shoulders. "You coming?"

"She's all yours, Patrick." Jake feigned indifference to the most interesting female that had entered this town in the last decade. He'd just have to wait to hear all the mystery woman details tonight at the Fireweed Café.

Annie still might have her sights set on him. And no way in the world was he voluntarily setting himself up for ridicule. Nor was he showing the slightest interest in a beautiful stranger. Following on the heels of Derek's embarrassing ad, Jake could just imagine the townsfolk's reaction to that.

He shuddered. Nope. For now he'd just head right on back to the ranch and finish off the new stallion pen, exactly as he'd planned.

THE SOUND OF HAMMERING reached Robin on her mother's back porch. She'd made herself scarce while her brother-in-law read a story to her nephews and Grandma settled down for a nap.

She was amazed by how much her three nephews had grown since last Christmas. She normally saw them twice a year when family gathered at her sister's cottage near Prince George for an old-fashioned Christmas then a lazy summer vacation. But this year they seemed to be on some kind of accelerated growth plan.

She smiled as she lowered herself into a wood slat chair. Grandma, however, hadn't aged a bit. Hugging her earlier in the familiar living room, Robin had felt eighteen years old again.

The house was the same. The yard was the same. Her gaze drifted across the acreage that was dominated by her mother's market garden, pausing on the shiny new barn on the property next door. The barn was a very big change.

She wondered how long it had been since the Bronsons had left town. When Old Man Bronson owned the property it had been an eyesore of tilting, rotting clapboard, rusted cars and weed-choked lawns. By contrast, the new owners had bulldozed the old junk, built a magnificent two-story log house, and planted oats and hay to feed the dozens of horses grazing in white-fenced paddocks.

Whoever bought the place certainly seemed to have money. Which made Robin wonder why they'd chosen a town like Forever.

As she mulled the question, a shirtless man strode around the corner of the barn. He wore a leather tool belt low on his faded jeans and held a hammer in his right hand. Sweat glistened on his chest and upper arms, emphasizing bulging muscles. A cowboy hat shaded his face.

"Magnificent" was the word that popped immediately into Robin's mind. If she ever decided on recreational sex, instead of serious procreation, this was exactly the kind of guy she'd go for.

She watched unblinking as he bent over one of the fence rails at the property line and drove a nail into it with three sure strokes. Then he straightened, holstered the hammer and stepped back to survey the section of fence. The sun caught his face as he tipped his chin up.

Jacob Bronson.

Robin froze.

It felt as if her heart had splatted against her backbone then ricocheted against her ribs before taking up a jerky rhythm that left her gasping for breath. She'd never expected to see him again.

He suddenly stilled, as if he'd caught her scent. Eyes narrowing, he looked straight at the covered porch.

He couldn't see her. Surely to goodness he couldn't see her in the shadow of the awning. And even if he could, he wouldn't recognize her, not from a hundred yards away after fifteen years.

So why did his blue-eyed stare seem to penetrate to her very soul? Her eyes fluttered closed against the unnerving sensation.

She wouldn't remember.

She *refused* to allow the humiliating memories to crowd her mind.

She'd successfully kept them at bay since the day she boarded the floatplane out of town fifteen years ago, and there was no reason for them to surface now. No reason at all—unless you counted a mere glimpse of the man who had witnessed her greatest folly. She groaned as recollections burst forth in crisp color and vivid detail.

It had happened more than fifteen years ago. The night before graduation when the twenty-one seniors of Forever Public School carried on the town tradition of skinny-dipping at Make-Out Beach. It was a rite of passage on the summer solstice when the midnight sun dipped briefly below the horizon and the water darkened just enough to preserve modesty.

Make-Out Beach was private and secluded. Ten

miles out of town, it was accessible only by a dirt road that wound along the riverbank, giving swimmers and anyone else ample notice of approaching visitors.

Robin had banished her fears that night and trooped down to the girls' beach with her friends to enter the water in privacy.

Modest and hesitant compared to many of her classmates, she'd deliberated for long minutes before she'd decided the voracious mosquitoes on shore were a greater evil than stripping naked and slipping into the icy water.

One by one the other girls had drifted over to join the boys. She could still hear shrieks and laughter above the crackling fire. It reflected orange off the slow-moving water just beyond the shrub-covered point that separated the two beaches. Even her friend, Annie, had inched her way around to the main beach.

Robin waded along the soft, sandy bottom and hugged her cool shoulders. She was being ridiculous. She couldn't just cower here all night long.

Everyone else seemed to be having fun. It didn't sound as though the boys were taking advantage. The shrieks and screams mostly coincided with a huge, brightly colored beach ball soaring high above the treetops.

She took a couple of strokes toward the point. She was all alone, and the chilled water rushed over her sensitive skin as she glided across the surface. She intended to peek around the corner, just to see what they were all doing. Maybe she could unobtrusively join in at the edge of the group.

Leafy wild cranberry bushes clung to the point of land that separated the two coves. She drifted toward the voices. As she neared the end of the point, she could see Rose out in the deep water. Seth and Alex were treading water in attendance, playfully splashing her from several feet away. Annie and three other girls clustered together, crouched in the shallows.

A mosquito bit Robin's neck. She slapped at it. Another stung her ear and she shook her head so her hair flung out in all directions. As if a signal had passed from bug to bug, she was suddenly surrounded by the whining insects. In danger of inhaling the pests, she ducked her head under the water and pushed away from the shore.

When she surfaced, the swarm quickly zeroed in on her again. Another deep breath and she was back under, swimming further away from the point, away from the voices and laughter, through the silent dark water. She didn't surface again until her lungs insisted.

Then she burst up out of the water, gasping. The bugs were gone, but the current had caught her and pulled her to the far side of the girls' beach. Robin sighed in exasperation, wishing she had just stayed home.

She stretched into a front crawl. She was a strong swimmer, but she made frustratingly slow progress through the cold water. It would be easier close to shore where the current was weak, but the memory of the hungry mosquitoes kept her twenty feet away from the bushes that harbored the swarms.

Her foot brushed a tree branch hidden under the water. It scraped and stung, and she gasped out loud. She put her feet down. Her toes squished through soft, sucking mud. She shuddered and jerked her feet back up, trying to not wonder about leeches.

She began rhythmically stroking through the water, thinking longingly of her big beach towel and Annie's truck with the rolled-up windows. She kicked out a little further from shore. Her foot hit another deadfall tree. As she jerked away, her ankle was suddenly wedged tight in a tangle of branches, pulling her briefly under the water.

Great. She quickly surfaced and maneuvered around to pull her foot out from the opposite direction. Her ankle wrenched with the movement and she gasped.

A mosquito buzzed next to her ear. She batted at it, then gingerly felt along the slimy log with her other foot. She found a solid purchase and sighed in relief, balancing herself with small arm movements.

Her trapped foot throbbed a bit, but she was pretty sure it wasn't seriously hurt. In any event, it was as good as packed in ice down there in the river water. She twisted it to the left. Nothing. Then she tried twisting it to the right. Still nothing.

She reached down along her bare leg until her hand found the branches. It was impossible to get a good grip without ducking her head under the water. So she ducked and pulled at the offending branch with all her strength.

It wouldn't bend. It wouldn't break. She surfaced again, wiping the water out of her eyes.

Should she call for help?

Wouldn't that just be the most entertaining moment of the entire senior year? Eight boys all pawing around her naked body, trying to be the hero. Robin shuddered.

How long was it until a person became hypothermic in glacial water? She couldn't remember what the first-aid manual said. Since she normally had total recall, was that a sign her brain was freezing?

She was overreacting. Goose bumps were forming on her skin and she was starting to shiver, but she was pretty sure she wasn't in any immediate danger.

She ducked under the water once again, using both hands to try to free her foot. When she burst back through the surface she was no better off. Robin swore under her breath.

"Need some help?"

She nearly screamed at the deep voice directly behind her. She twisted around.

Jacob Bronson. The class geek. A rangy, slouch-shouldered, slow-talkin' boy from the poorest family in town. His jeans were always too short, and he missed more school than he attended, working the pathetic piece of ground his father liked to call a farm.

"Uh." She chewed her lip. It was pretty obvious

she needed help here. And she didn't *think* Jacob was dangerous. He might try to cop a feel, but then, so would Seth or Alex given the opportunity.

She was known as the Ice Princess because of her standoffish airs and habit of keeping all the boys at arm's length. Though, in truth, it was more fear than superiority that kept her virtuous. Not that her reasons mattered. She could well imagine the prestigious bragging rights a guy would have for sliding his hands over a buck-naked Robin Medford in a rescue attempt.

Better one boy without an audience, she decided. One quiet boy at that. Though she strongly suspected even Jacob would break his silence to talk about this one.

It was settled then. Jacob was going to run his big rough hands along her naked legs.

She looked nervously up into his charcoal-blue eyes. He wasn't laughing at her or leering at her. In fact, he looked genuinely concerned. She swallowed.

Her voice quavered as she answered his question. "Yes. Please."

JACOB'S HANDS were gentle as they encircled her ankle. Of necessity, his cheek was in close proximity to her navel under the water.

She gazed up at the pale blue sky where a faint quarter moon bravely attempted to shine despite the midnight sun hovering just below the distant mountains. She tried valiantly to pretend this wasn't happening.

Jacob's cheek brushed her abdomen. She sucked in a frantic breath as a strange humming sensation worked its way along her limbs. The pressure of the tree branch lessened for a second, then snapped back. Robin jerked from the brief flash of pain.

Jacob surfaced. "Sorry."

She shook her head. "It's okay." He was trying to be gentle, she could tell. She stared straight at his naked chest, wondering if succumbing to hypothermia might not be a better way to go. She was never going to live this down.

He clamped his jaw. "I'm, uh, going to have to..."

"What?" Please, oh, please, don't let him go for help.

"Well...you see..." He raked a hand through his short-cropped hair. "I'll have to wrap my arms around your leg..."

"So?" She was just relieved that he wasn't going for an audience. She was beginning to worry that Annie would come looking for her.

"Just hurry," she implored.

"Okay. I'm sorry." He ducked under the water again.

The freshening breeze tangled her wet hair, chilling her face and scalp. She could feel his strong arms working their way around, no, *between* her legs. Her eyes widened.

His shoulder brushed her upper thighs. Her body hummed again. It felt... It felt...

She closed her eyes as her entire body seemed to convulse with longing. His fingers surrounded her ankle and his shoulder flexed enticingly. Then suddenly his body was rushing along the length of her, coming up for air.

He stood completely still, looking intently past her right ear at the black-green bushes on shore as he sucked in long breaths. Robin stared up at the droplets of water clinging to his dark, thick lashes. She felt flushed, warm, itchy. Her lips parted.

Suddenly she was in no hurry to get free. She wanted him to rub against her legs again. She liked the feel of his skin, the friction of the water.

He glanced hotly into her eyes for a split second before he dove. Abandoning any pretense of keeping their body contact to a minimum, his strong, sure hands explored her ankle and the branches surrounding it. His shoulders, neck and hair alternately rubbed and brushed her inner thighs and higher.

Her knees felt weak, and she reached down tentatively to steady herself. She touched his square shoulders, the shifting steel of his muscles, and suddenly felt safe. Here, trapped and naked in the Forever River, rubbing up against Jacob Bronson, and she'd never felt so secure in her life.

His ragged clothes and perpetual slouch had hidden a magnificent sinewy physique. Unable to stop herself, she let her hands slide down his upper arms.

Bulging biceps flexed under her touch. His cheek rested against the top of her thigh, chin just barely brushing the downy curls.

Robin's entire world focused on that insubstantial touch.

She felt her ankle slip free.

As he slowly surfaced she let her hands move with him, keeping her grip on his arms, telling herself it was so she wouldn't fall.

She gazed into his eyes, then noted for the first time his coarse beard stubble. It was a marked contrast to the sparse facial hair of the other boys in the class. He was really quite handsome, in a rugged, dangerous sort of way. She wondered why she hadn't noticed before.

His big hands gently closed around her rib cage and she realized her breasts were out of the water, puckered and exposed to his avid gaze. She shuddered, but made no move to conceal herself. A coyote howled on the mountainside. Its pups answered in short yips.

He was going to kiss her. She could see the longing in his eyes.

The longing transformed to determination, then resolve.

He slowly bent forward.

She tipped her head to accommodate him. His cold lips touched her softly. They warmed against her own. They opened. She followed suit, and his tongue pushed through. He tasted of mint and smelled faintly of spiced aftershave long diluted by the river water.

His arms wound slowly, inexorably, around her, and she pressed her long fingernails into his taut shoulder muscles, desperate to get closer. She felt him brace himself on the bottom against the rushing current. He was strong and sure and invincible.

He lifted her, holding her naked body flush against his own. She wound her arms around his neck, and felt her legs begin to encircle his hips. Steadying herself, she rationalized.

The roar of the river pounded in her ears. If there were any mosquitoes lingering, she sure didn't feel them. All sensation was centered inside; hot pulsating waves of hormones propelling her toward the unknown.

He left her mouth and she whimpered in disappointment. But then he kissed her neck, slipped his hands lower to cup her bottom, and she tightened her knees against his hips.

"Robin?" His voice sounded strangled.

"Yes?" she hissed. A knot of tension coiled tighter and tighter inside her until all she wanted...all she needed...

He stroked one hand over the back of her head, pulling her tight against his shoulder. "You don't want this."

"What?" What was he talking about? She wanted this more than she'd ever wanted anything in her life.

She was his for the taking. He was beautiful and bold. He was the boy—no, the man—she'd waited for.

"Robin," he rasped. "We have to stop."

"No." She burrowed her face into the crook of his neck, using her tongue to test the tiny droplets of water clinging there. He was delicious.

He pulled back with a gasp, thwarting her efforts. He looked her straight in the eye. There was intelligence, clarity and determination in that gaze. "You do not want this to happen."

He was sending her away.

She slowly shook her head in an effort to stop him.

When he spoke again his harsh whisper was precise and implacable. "You're Robin Medford. I'm Jacob Bronson. You do *not* want this to happen."

She felt tears well up behind her eyes and she banged her clenched fist against his shoulder.

Because he was so right.

And because he was also so very wrong....

"Robin?"

It took her a split second to realize his voice was in the present, not the past.

She lifted her lashes to stare into the same pair of charcoal-blue eyes.

He hadn't told a soul.

2

JAKE MET the confused vulnerability in Robin's expression and had to steel himself against a wash of memories. The last time she'd looked at him that way she'd been naked in his arms, forcing him to use every single scrap of strength and valor he possessed to keep from making love to her.

In an instant he was transported back in time, to the beach, to the night before graduation. He swore he could hear the rush of the river, smell her lemon perfume, and feel her wet, silken skin heating under his fingertips.

The screen door opened with a bang.

"Robin?" Connie, Robin's older sister and a frequent visitor to Forever, stepped onto the porch. "Oh, hi, Jake. Finished work for the day?"

Jake forced his gaze away from Robin and cleared his mind of the bewitching memories. He'd never been back to that beach. Not once.

He took a sharp, bracing breath of the evening air. Personal ads, marriage proposals—just when he thought life couldn't get more surreal, Forever's mystery woman turned out to be Robin Medford.

"I'm all done." He answered Connie's question.

"Jacob Bronson?" Robin seemed to come back to life. She laughed lightly, tucking her sandy-blond hair behind one ear with a trembling hand. "I didn't recognize you at first."

Well, wasn't that just a boost to a guy's ego? He'd been fantasizing about the woman for fifteen years, and she didn't even remember him. Perfect.

"Grandma wants you to stay for dinner, Jake," said Connie.

He supposed he should be gratified that at least one sister knew who he was. Connie pushed the sleeves of her multicoloured sweatshirt to her elbows and crossed her arms. Though she was only four years his senior, she had a habit of treating him as if he were one of her children.

"I don't want to intrude." He seized on a perfectly legitimate excuse to make himself scarce. Robin's presence meant the entire Medford clan was together for the first time in several years. They probably wanted to be alone. Jake sure wanted them to be alone.

He'd have to be a very masochistic man to voluntarily sit across the dinner table from her. The woman didn't even *remember* the kisses that had rocked his adolescent world and resonated for a decade and a half.

"Don't be silly," Connie said breezily, opening the door wider and gesturing for them to enter. "You're practically family."

With a small smile, Robin gracefully rose from the

chair. She didn't echo her sister's invitation—probably because she didn't care whether he stayed or not.

As she strolled toward the kitchen door, her wavy hair bounced and the worn denim jeans molded to her sexy thighs. His fingertips tingled with a tactile memory of those curves. He wrapped his hands into fists. From what he could see, her body hadn't changed a bit.

He forced himself to curb the hormonal reaction. She hadn't changed since graduation, not in looks and not in character. To her, he was still Jacob Bronson, class geek. And the Ice Princess was just as remote now as she'd ever been.

It was time to take a serious look at that stack of letters from the personal ad. Derek was right. Jake should hurry up and find a suitable wife. Then he could exorcise Robin from his psyche once and for all.

It was the logical thing to do—the safe thing to do. But as the woman of his dreams disappeared around the corner, all thoughts of logic and safety evaporated. And he knew if he didn't get the heck out of Dodge this minute, he was in big, big trouble.

He glanced swiftly at Connie, hoping she hadn't noticed the way his gaze lingered on Robin's rear end. He raked a hand through his hair. "Sorry, Connie, but I can't—"

"Grandma is *not* going to take no for an answer, Jake. You work too hard. Now get over there and find yourself a decent shirt. If you're not back in five minutes I'm sending the boys after you."

He shook his head. "Really, I—"

"I'll send them over," she threatened with a resolute lift of her chin. "And Grandma will be upset with you."

He yielded to the inevitable with an inward sigh. "Yes, ma'am." He definitely didn't want to upset Alma May so close to her big birthday. And Connie's boys, at eight, six and four, were capable of doing serious damage to the inside of his house.

The thought of pacifying his housekeeper after another round of the three musketeers was more than a little daunting. Sexy Robin versus an upset housekeeper. Definitely a no-win situation.

Connie's indomitable stare tipped the balance to Robin's side. Fine. He'd stay for dinner and make the best of it. Maybe if he worked her out of his system up front, he could cope with the rest of her visit. Then maybe he could get on with the rest of his life.

IT WASN'T HAPPENING. With Robin directly across the dinner table, he was definitely *not* working her out of his system. In fact, as her moist lips parted in another affectionate smile, she was rapidly working her way right back in. Sure, all that charm was directed toward her nephews, but Jake's psyche didn't seem to care.

He thought he'd had it bad in high school, but right now his lust meter was about to blow off the charts.

"Were they real lions, Auntie Robin?" Connie's youngest son's eyes widened.

Robin's straight white teeth flashed in the candlelight. "They were real, Bobby," she answered. Her
finger absently traced the gold rim of her saucer as
she recounted a recent trip to Kenya. "A mommy
lion, a daddy and two cubs."

"Were you scared?" Next to Jake, Bobby put down
his dessert spoon and leaned forward.

"A little bit," said Robin. Her blue-green eyes
danced in a way that made Jake's skin tingle. Their
depth and clarity reminded him of the Forever River.
"But we were inside the truck. So we were safe."

Connie cleared her throat. "Any *other* adventures
you can tell us about before bed, Robin?" she asked
pointedly. "I don't suppose you've been to an amusement park lately."

Robin picked up on her sister's warning tone and
smoothly switched gears to a less nightmare-inciting
subject. "As a matter of fact." She flipped her long
hair back out of the way and started to remove her
sweater in the warm room. "I haven't been to any
amusement parks. But I've always wanted to go
down a water slide."

Her confession brought an instant high-cut bikini
visual to Jake's mind and he shifted in his chair.

"We went on water slides last summer," said
Bobby on a near squeal.

"You did?" She did a credible imitation of surprise.
"Why don't you tell me about them?"

As Bobbie and his brothers chatted on, Robin finished removing her sweater and hung it on the back

of her chair. Jake's vision narrowed to a tunnel, and the boys' voices faded to a faraway roar.

Her smoothly tanned shoulders and long graceful neck were revealed by a sleeveless white tank top. A gold locket danced against the scooped neckline as she moved. And the clingy fabric of the shirt delineated her breasts.

Jake's memory kicked in, and he couldn't help visualizing her breasts in excruciating detail. Sure it had been pretty dark, but he'd seem them once. Pale, full, coral-tipped, tight from the chilly water droplets that clung to her supple skin.

Oh, yeah. He'd seen them once. And that was more than any other man in Forever could lay claim to.

Not that Jake would ever lay that claim. He'd never even contemplated laying that claim. Well, except the one time. And he figured he could be forgiven for that particular impulse.

It was the day after they'd gone skinny-dipping. At the dinner following the convocation ceremony in the school gymnasium. Robin had sat there on a folding chair, as cool and composed as the Ice Princess she was reputed to be.

She'd swept her hair up, and wispy curls framed her face. Her makeup was subtle and flattering, and her snug black, spaghetti-strapped dress showed off high, pert breasts and softly rounded hips. She was the stuff teenage dreams were made of. At least she was the stuff Jake's dreams were made of.

As he'd watched her from across the room, he'd

willed her to glance his way, to make some small gesture to say he was no longer persona non grata in her eyes. He just wanted a small sign that she'd appreciated his chivalrous behavior.

He'd sat there alone in the ill-fitting worn suit he'd pilfered from his father's closet. He entertained wild fantasies that she'd approach him, speak to him, privately thank him for calling a halt the night before, and let it be known they were friends.

But she hadn't. And for one crazy second he'd been tempted to swagger over to Seth and Alex and the rest of the boys to recount it all.

She wouldn't have denied it, couldn't have denied it. Everyone in town knew that Robin's neck turned bright red whenever she told less than the truth. He could have elevated his social status to the stratosphere with a few well-chosen sentences.

It was a big temptation for a misfit eighteen-year-old boy. But the thirty-two-year-old man was inordinately proud of his silence.

Across the dinner table, she laughed at something the children said. It had been the most noble moment of his life. Too bad she didn't even remember.

"YOU MUST REMEMBER what that overpowering maternal urge feels like." Robin pegged one of her nephew's T-shirts on the clothesline behind her mother's house. She ran her hand lovingly across the damp fabric of the tiny garment. Soon, she told herself. Soon she'd have tiny clothes of her own to wash.

"But I was already married," said Connie. "I had somebody to support me and help me."

"I don't need anybody to support me." Money was not an issue. "My promotion at Wild Ones will keep me in one city, and the salary is enough for anything we might need." Including teeny, tiny clothes.

"I don't just mean financial support." Connie draped a voluminous bedsheet over the line. "I mean emotional support."

"In case you've forgotten, I'm a very independent person." Her job as a location scout for Wild Ones Tours took her all over the globe. She traveled alone, checking out potential adventure tours for the company to promote. She enjoyed the freedom.

"Well, you've never *independently* paced the floor at 2:00 a.m. with a crying baby in your arms."

"I once stayed up for forty-eight hours straight, pacing nervously while I listened to lions roar." She could handle sleep deprivation and emotional fatigue.

"It's not the same thing." Then Connie grinned. "Though it might be good training."

"See?" Robin added a peg to an end of the bedsheet, smoothing out the wrinkles with the palm of her hand. "I'm completely ready."

"But the lions went away after forty-eight hours. Babies stay for years."

"I know that." Robin had considered her plan from all angles. She loved babies. She loved children. She was not going to end up a decrepit old maiden aunt to Connie's boys just because she hadn't met the right man during her child-bearing years.

"I'm only suggesting you wait a bit. You never know what's right around the corner in life."

"I'm thirty-two years old. The window of opportunity is closing. Have you read the statistics for child-bearing past thirty-five?"

"Women have babies as late as forty now."

"It's a much higher risk."

"You read too much."

"How old were you when you had Sammy?"

"Twenty-eight."

"See."

"But I was married."

"This isn't 1950. Women do not have to define their lives by their marital status." Robin believed that. She really did. Sure, she'd like a father for her children. But she'd worked in more than thirty countries around the world, she'd met men of all shapes, sizes, ideologies and personalities. She'd never once found one she wanted to spend her life with.

She wasn't getting married simply to be married.

"What are you going to tell Grandma?" Connie pegged up the last pillowcase and lifted the empty laundry basket, settling it at her waist.

"I haven't decided yet." Robin bit her lower lip, fixing a small wrinkle in the pillowcase. "I'll probably make up a temporary boyfriend."

"So she won't know you had casual sex?" Connie quirked her eyebrows.

Robin hesitated. She wasn't at all comfortable lying to her grandmother, but she was even less comfortable telling her the truth. "There'll be nothing casual about it. It will be deliberate and effective."

"Let me guess." Connie turned and started for the short staircase. "You've read a book on this, too."

"Of course." Robin followed. "I've researched fertility and conception." She had a basal body thermometer in her suitcase. She'd done her first temperature test run last month, and was doing another this month. She could identify her fertile time to within twenty-four hours.

Connie laughed. "I just hope you make sure your baby reads the same books you did. They tend to ignore the experts and do whatever the heck they want."

"I read that, too."

"Of course you did."

"I'm ready for this," Robin assured her sister. "I'm probably more ready for this than most married women."

Connie sighed. Then she turned and lowered herself to sit on the stairs, setting the basket on the dry grass beside her.

"You know, you don't *always* have to grab life by the throat and shake it until it gives you what you want."

"That was a ridiculously obscure statement." Intrigued, Robin sat next to her big sister.

"You've always been like that."

"Like what?"

"Once you set your sights on the goal line, you don't look to the right or to the left. You just blast along like a steamroller."

"I'm efficient. I get things done." There was nothing worse than wandering willy-nilly around an idea for months on end. Once you made a decision, you implemented it. Simple as that.

Connie leaned over and picked a blade of grass, twisting it in her fingertips. "Take Wild Ones, for instance. You decided working as a location scout for an adventure travel company was a great way to see the world."

"It was." Robin wasn't getting her sister's point. Her career with Wild Ones was an ongoing success. As an example of mistakes in life, it was rather pathetic.

"They needed pilots. You became a pilot."

"So?"

"They needed translators. You learned Portuguese."

"I don't understand what you're getting at. What's wrong with learning Portuguese? These are all good things."

"Everything you did, for years and years, was focused toward the goal of becoming a perfect Wild Ones employee."

"I still don't see this as a problem. So I'm focused? So I'm determined? It's taken me a long way in life."

A gust of wind blew Robin's hair across her face, and she swept the strands behind her ear.

"But you never give life a chance."

"A chance to do what?"

"You never trust that there are people around you who might make good things happen. Good things that you never even knew you wanted. All I'm suggesting is that you slow down for a while and give fate a chance."

Fate? Robin had tried fate once. Fifteen years ago in the Forever River. But Jacob Bronson had stopped her, thank goodness.

She still shuddered at the possible consequences of making love with Jake. She might have become pregnant at eighteen. Or worse, she might have imagined she was in love with him and stayed in Forever. She would have missed out on her education, her career, her *life*.

No. Fate couldn't be trusted in the driver's seat.

She blinked at Connie. "You want me to wander willy-nilly through life and let fate blow me around like a dried leaf?"

"It's worked for me. I never would have met Robert if I hadn't missed that plane to Seattle."

"That was luck."

"Call it what you want."

"I don't know, Connie. I can't imagine myself hanging around international airports hoping to meet the man of my dreams."

Connie chuckled. "All I'm suggesting is that you

go with the flow once in a while. Let the wind take you."

"Like a dried leaf?"

"You're not a dried leaf." Connie sighed and put an arm around Robin. "Just don't get so focused that you miss an opportunity right under your nose."

"I'll try." Robin's gaze relaxed on the honey-warm logs of Jake's new house. She and fate did not have a good track record.

"But whatever you decide," said Connie. "You know you'll have my full support."

Robin's chest constricted. She blinked quickly. "Thanks."

"Mom!" Bobby shrieked from inside. "Sammy broke my truck."

"Did not."

"Did, too."

"Did not."

"In the meantime, think long and hard about having those kids." Connie shook her head as she trotted up the stairs.

THE BOYS' ARGUMENT subsided, and distant laughter drifted over from Jake's property. Robin brought his house back into focus. Jake and three other people, two men and a woman, strolled past a neat row of square, quarter-acre horse pens.

She watched his confident, long-legged stride, and thought about fate. Had fate brought him to her that night in the river? Was it fate that had made her want him or fate that had made him stop?

Would she have become pregnant? Would she have fallen in love?

She shook herself. It was irrelevant, really. Since they couldn't go back to find out.

Jake and his friends stopped beside a central corral. The chestnut stallion penned up inside circled, snorted and kicked exuberantly in the cool morning air.

Robin knew she should follow her sister and help make lunch for the kids, but she couldn't take her eyes off Jake. He'd more than fulfilled the physical promise she glimpsed back then. Hard-muscled, he moved his big body with athletic grace and ease. If he ever wanted to leave Forever, she could probably get him a job at Wild Ones. Maybe he could model for their adventure brochures.

He swung up to the top fence rail, then tipped back his Stetson hat and raised his fingers to his mouth, emitting a shrill whistle. Horses from all over the ranch perked up their ears. There was a general shift of horseflesh in his direction. Robin stepped forward for a better view.

Good grief, she was just as bad as the horses.

The stallion in the corral cantered over, switching back and forth in front of Jake. Jake slowly lowered himself to the ground inside the corral. The people around him closed in and he was lost to view.

Then he was back. He was up on the horse. Hat settled firmly on his head, biceps bulging beneath his white T-shirt, he touched its flanks with his boot heels and the animal sprang off the ground.

Robin gasped, fighting an urge to rush forward.

The horse's body arced. It came down hard, front hooves sending up a cloud of dust that gusted sideways across the pen. Then it immediately kicked its back legs toward the sky, haunch and shoulder muscles bunched and shifting with its rage.

Was the man out of his *mind*?

Jake's sinewy muscles kept perfect pace with the angry animal. As he leaned back and elongated his body, Robin unconsciously tightened her muscles with him. His free arm trailed out to one side, rocking against the empty air in time to the movements of the horse. The horse's hind legs barely touched the earth before they rebounded again. Each leap was higher than the last.

She willed him to stick to the animal's back.

It changed tactics, crow-hopping sideways toward the fence as if it intended to scrape Jake off. She inched closer, pressing her legs together, as if the force of her concentration would help him stay put.

He held his seat. His rear end alternately connected with the horse's bare back and defied physics by hovering above the shifting target as if they were cosmically connected.

The horse took a sudden twist. Several of its cohorts whinnied in apparent excitement and approval as Jake's hat hit the dirt. Robin's legs moved under her, quickening into a jog, stopping only when she came to the fence that separated the two properties. She gripped the smooth, painted rails, gaze riveted to the spectacle, prepared to leap over and use her first-aid skills if need be.

She cringed as the horse twisted again. Just when she thought Jake would win, the animal jerked to one side. Jake's butt came down a split second too late. He clutched the air, then sprawled, facedown, sending up a dense cloud of brown dust.

Had he hit his head? It looked as if he'd hit his head.

Robin vaulted over the fence. The riderless horse bucked away, its mouth frothing and sweat glistening on its flanks. Sprinting across the field, she focused on Jake's crumpled body.

Before she made it halfway, Jake leaped to his feet. He limped toward the agitated horse, stopping part way to lean down and retrieve his battered hat. He whacked it against his leg before settling it back on his head.

Robin kept running as he moved closer and closer to the wild animal. He held up his hands, speaking in a hollow, soothing baritone. The man was truly insane. The horse didn't look soothed, it looked menacing and angry as it snorted and pawed the ground.

Still, Jake moved closer. Her mind raced. When was the last time she'd set a broken bone? Did the small Forever hospital have a doctor on site at all times?

When he came within arm's reach of the wide-eyed beast, it stilled, twitching its ears and shaking its head. Robin cringed, preparing for a sudden flash of sharp hooves or snapping teeth.

On the opposite side of the corral, the three strangers noted her approach and smiled happily at her. They behaved as if they hadn't a care in the world. Gasping for breath, she stopped at the raw wood fence of the corral.

To her surprise, the horse didn't attack. Quite the contrary, it nuzzled Jake's shirt pocket until he produced something that the horse promptly ate.

Robin rocked back on her heels. She had obviously missed something here. She was the only one who seemed even remotely upset. And that included the horse.

The audience burst into spontaneous applause. Jake turned toward them, removed his hat, and gave a deep bow. That sure didn't seem like the action of a man who'd just defied death. He pushed his dark, wavy hair back off his forehead before replacing the hat.

Robin glanced from side to side, wishing she could slink back over the property line. Rodeo Jake had just been entertaining the crowd.

The youngest and tallest of the three spectators made his way around the corral toward Robin. He stopped in front of her and offered his hand. "Derek Sullivan. I'm a friend of Jake's."

"Robin Medford." She accepted the neatly dressed

man's handshake. Nothing to do but brazen it out. Maybe they'd all assume she'd come over to watch the show.

He looked to be about her own age, but he definitely hadn't grown up in Forever.

"Nice horse," she said, nodding toward the animal, pretending she had a clue what she was talking about. Jake started across the corral toward them, his worn cowboy boots sinking in the soft dirt with each step.

"Dynamo's as good as they come."

If that was the case, Robin sure didn't want to see a bad horse. "Is this what he does for entertainment?"

"Dynamo?"

"Jake."

Derek grinned. "Only as a favor to me."

Derek *wanted* Jake to get tossed off a wild bucking horse? Some friend. She glanced at the older couple. They had wandered over to admire a mare and foal.

"Hey, Robin." Jake nodded, eyes narrowing quizzically as he came to a stop and placed one booted foot on the bottom rail. He probably wondered what she was doing here, since she'd made such a point of *not* engaging him in conversation last night. He wiped the sweat from his forehead with the back of his hand.

She wondered what the heck she was doing here, too. Her memories of their teenage encounter were so fresh and vivid, she actually felt embarrassed looking him in the eye. And she felt attracted. As attracted as she'd been fifteen years ago.

"Hi," she returned, swallowing to combat the breathy sound of her voice. Dust didn't usually turn her on. Neither did sweat, faded jeans or well-worn cowboy boots.

Jake cocked his head sideways, his expression becoming almost hesitant. "So, what did you think of the ride?"

Frightening. Insane. Gorgeous. Sexy. "The horse seemed a bit...frisky."

Both men chuckled.

"We like 'em that way," Derek offered.

"To each his own." Robin wished her pulse rate would return to normal.

"You do know what I do for a living, right?" asked Jake.

"Not exactly." She forced herself to concentrate on the lone cloud developing above the mountain peak. She knew he raised horses, but hadn't given much thought to what he did with them in Forever. Tourist trail riding, she supposed. With really healthy tourists.

"I raise rodeo horses."

"Rodeo horses? In Forever?" Her gaze zipped from the cloud to his face.

"Right here in Forever," he said.

"Thanks for the demo, buddy." Derek clapped Jake on the shoulder, releasing a small cloud of dust. Tiny particles clung to Jake's face, accenting his beard stubble and highlighting the interesting lines crinkling the corners of his charcoal-blue eyes.

"See you later tonight. Nice to meet you, Robin." Derek headed over to collect the older couple.

Jake waved his friend off with a nod.

He ducked between the fence rails, then straightened and leaned back, crossing his boots at the ankles. His familiar eyes caressed her, sending the pulse in her throat into overdrive. "So, Robin, what can I do for you?"

Several answers immediately blossomed in her mind. None of which she could voice.

3

"NOTHING," was what she quickly said. "I mean, I, uh..." She didn't want him to think she was here to rekindle the old flame. But she didn't want to talk about her Florence Nightingale impulse, either.

"Nice place you've got here," she offered a bit desperately, glancing around the ranch. Close up, she was truly dazzled by what he'd done with his family's land.

Connie had raved about his hard work and vision. Looking at the house, the barn, pens and outbuildings, Robin could certainly understand why. It must have taken some kind of work ethic over the past fifteen years to accomplish all of this.

He peered at her from under his hat brim, recapturing her attention. "So you came over to admire the place?"

"Yeah." She nodded and immediately felt her neck heat up.

He looked pointedly and skeptically at her open shirt collar, then returned his gaze to her face, raising his eyebrows. "Did you come over to watch me ride?"

"Yeah."

His eyes narrowed, and he reached forward to tip her collar out of the way. "Want me to ask you something really embarrassing?"

"No!"

He let go of her collar without the slightest brush to her skin. She couldn't stop a little flare of disappointment. Those calloused hands were a real turn-on. Of course, so was pretty much everything else about him.

He chuckled, shaking his head. "Just tell me why you're here."

Robin sighed with exasperation. She hated that built-in lie detector. There were definite disadvantages to being around people who'd known her as a child. "I thought you might need medical attention."

He pulled back. "You're not a doctor."

"I'm a licensed paramedic."

"You're kidding."

"People don't tend to joke about that."

"That's not what I meant." The horse trotted past behind him, nickering softly, obviously none the worse for wear. "I'm just surprised, that's all. I thought you were doing wilderness tours."

"I was. Well, I was scouting locations, anyway. It helps to have medical training when you're out in the field."

"That makes sense." A small silence followed his nod.

An errant blackfly buzzed her face, and she waved it away. She knew she should say goodbye and go help Connie with lunch. But she hesitated. Jake the Cowboy was everything Jake the Teenager had been, and more. He was all grown-up now, and so was she.

She couldn't help wondering what would happen if they met for a midnight swim at thirty-two instead of eighteen. Would he send her away this time?

She took half a step closer, eyeing the broad shoulders straining beneath his denim shirt. She itched to touch him, to see what his muscles felt like, hardened by time and ripened through experience.

She cleared her throat. "Do all your horses buck people off?" It was difficult to keep an inconsequential conversation going through her escalating sexual buzz.

"Not all of them." The gravelly base of his voice and the whisper of the wind reminded her they were alone. "I have a few that are rideable."

"Oh. Good. That's good."

"Would you like to try one?" he asked.

"A horse?"

"No, a bull." He grinned and her stomach flipped over. "Do you ride?"

It took her a second to recover her voice. "Yes. Yes, I ride horses. The nonbucking kind. Wild Ones Tours was considering a seven-day trek in Brazil last year."

"So you tested it out."

"Yeah."

"Well, this isn't Brazil." He angled his head toward the towering hills behind his ranch. "But I have a little bay mare who needs some exercise, if you'd like to take a ride up the back."

"With you?"

"With me."

Her legs weakened at the thought. Or maybe they were weak from the long run. Who could tell? "Just the two of us?"

"Unless you think we need a chaperone," he joked. But when his eyes caught hers, his smile swiftly faded.

The awakenings that had coursed through her young body pulsed with a vengeance.

He stilled. The air around him hummed with raw energy.

Oh, boy.

Was Connie right? Was this how fate reached out and grabbed you?

It was too early for her to be fertile. So fate obviously didn't want Jake to father her child. Maybe fate just wanted them to have great sex.

"Sure." She smiled. "I'll go riding with you."

JAKE TETHERED THE HORSES on a small, green plateau high above Forever where an underground stream surfaced for a few feet then disappeared into a rock fissure. So much for his master plan.

Staying close to Robin was easy. He'd sure been up close and personal in his dreams last night. It was the working-her-out-of-his-system part that had flaws.

Take now, for instance. The close part was on track.

She was only ten feet away, taking in the view of the river far below. Unfortunately, lust screamed from every pore in his body. And he wanted nothing more than to toss her down on the bed of wildflowers and see how long it took before her kisses completely blew his mind, ruining him for any other woman on the planet.

"Ever climbed the face?" She stepped up to the cliff edge, leaning forward to look over.

Jake closed the gap instinctively, ready to pull her to safety if need be. Then he remembered her career. She'd probably peered over the edge of mountain cliffs too numerous to mention.

The woman wasn't in any danger. He'd be the one committing suicide if he pulled her backward into the cradle of his hips.

"Seems like a waste of time and energy," he answered on a forced drawl, trapping his thumbs in his belt loops to keep his hands where they belonged.

"You think so?" She cocked her head sideways, considering the steep plunge. "I think I could sell this trip to Wild Ones."

"Yeah?"

"Horseback riding. Mountain climbing. River rafting. Who knows, someday Forever could be the adventure tourism mecca of the Yukon." She grinned and stepped away from the edge.

And then maybe you'd move back? He closed his eyes and shook his head, disgusted with himself. If he wasn't careful, he'd fall in love with her all over again. Then he'd have to stand helplessly by while she boarded the Beaver and stomped his heart to dust.

"You climb?" he asked.

She shrugged her small shoulders. "I took some lessons in Switzerland, but I've never done any of the big climbs."

"Big climbs?"

"Everest, the Matterhorn, K-2."

Her words highlighted the rift between their lifestyles. As if it needed any highlighting.

She took a few steps into the meadow and flopped down among the tiny kinnikinnick bushes and the Arctic poppies. Even in blue jeans and a cotton blouse, she looked exotic and out of place in a plain old sub-Arctic meadow. Robin and Forever never did fit.

He crouched a safe distance away, picking a couple of low-bush cranberries and popping them into his mouth. Their tart juice filled his mouth as he bit through the translucent skins.

She flashed a smile that made his insides twist like a sidewinding bronc on its first leap out of the chute. "Besides, hang gliding's a lot more fun and a lot less work."

"You've been hang gliding?" It was really easy to feel intimidated by this woman.

"Can't test an adventure vacation without having the adventure."

"What about bungee jumping?" he joked.

She grinned wider. "Tried it once. Didn't like it."

"Why not?" He certainly had no desire to jump off a bridge and dangle like a fish on a line. But nothing seemed too wild for Robin.

She picked an orange poppy and twirled it between her fingertips. The thin petals fanned outward. Her eyes danced as she replied. "Hard on the breasts."

He choked out a laugh. It was either that or groan as he pushed her to the ground and filled his palms with the objects under discussion. "That's probably more detail than I needed."

She tucked the flower behind her ear with a saucy grin. "Sorry."

"No problem." Yeah, right. No problem at all, except she was practically killing him. His fingers toyed with another berry, wishing he could feed it to her, then taste the rich, red juice on her lips.

Her smile faded as she gazed at a pair of eagles hanging on the air currents above the river.

"You never left," she said, looking back at him. For the first time since he'd startled her last night on the porch, there was nothing guarded in her expression.

"You never came back," he countered softly.

"Forever's a long way off the beaten track. And I see everyone at Connie's all the time." Her eyes seemed to reach down into his soul. The years fell away between them. "And I'm back now."

"But you're not staying." Were they having the

conversation he thought they were having? Was she broaching the subject of their relationship?

"No, I'm not staying," she said.

But? Was there a *but in the meantime* in that statement?

"What about you?" she continued, glancing away again. "Don't you ever wonder what's beyond those mountains?"

He blinked. He must have imagined the intimacy in her expression. Apparently they were only talking geography.

"No, I don't."

"Why not?" There was no censure in her voice, just plain curiosity.

"I already know what's beyond those mountains."

"Doesn't it make you want to reach out and grab it?"

He wasn't sure if he could make her understand how he felt about Forever. But he was willing to give it a try. He pointed to a flock of trumpeter swans gliding down to settle on a bend in the river, their distinctive voices filling the air. "How many places in the world have that?"

"Not many," she conceded. "But you've seen those all your life. Other places have other wonders—unique, exhilarating wonders." She shifted so she was kneeling, resting her rear on the backs of her heels, facing him. Blue-hot excitement burned in her eyes.

"You can't even imagine what it's like to see the

sun set on a hot lonely beach over the South Pacific. Poof." She threw her hands in the air, fingers extended. "A massive ball of orange flame that sinks like a stone into the black ocean. And the lions at midnight on the Serengeti plain. Their roar fills you with terror and awe." She hugged herself as if she were remembering a treasured moment.

Robin might be only two feet away, but her spirit was halfway around the world. He'd been a fool to dream about her for the past fifteen years. Keeping her in Forever would be like trying to cage a rainbow.

He should walk away, end it here and now, go home and start reading that stack of letters. He needed a real wife, not some intangible vision that breezed through his life every decade or so and left a quivering mass of frustration in her wake.

"You could leave, you know." Her pupils dilated. "Escape like I did."

He tensed. Of course he could leave. He might be a small-town man, but he wasn't naive. Did she think he hadn't noticed the floatplane taking off three times a week?

"You've obviously saved enough money," she continued, oblivious to his developing irritation. "Why don't you do it? Why don't you get out?"

He shook his head, telling himself she deserved his pity not his anger. If she couldn't find joy right here in Forever, she might not find it anywhere. "You're assuming one of my goals in life is to get out of this town."

"Well, I can't imagine your goal is to stay."

His jaw clenched. "This town's been good to me, Robin."

She frowned, wrinkling her forehead. "I was here, remember? This town was never good to you."

"The kids at school were never good to me." He didn't add that she was one of them. They both knew that.

He slid his gaze away from her as he spoke. Thunderheads clustered around the distant mountains and the smell of rain drifted in on the breeze. "The town was great to me."

"How so?" There was skepticism in her voice.

"Mrs. Wheeler, down at the bakery. She made up some story about having to cut the edges off her squares, couldn't sell the end pieces, she told me. All the boys eat them, she said. For twelve years she stood on her porch and handed me a bag of baking as I walked to school." Mrs. Wheeler still lived above the bakery. And Jake still visited her every week.

"I didn't know that."

"Of course you didn't. And Mrs. Henderson. Mrs. Henderson always managed to order a pair of jeans or a shirt that was a bit too small for Tommy Junior."

"She gave them to you?"

"She gave them to my mother, pretending we were doing her a big favor by taking them off her hands. Too much trouble to ship them out again. No point in paying that restocking charge to a big corporation, she'd say."

"Oh." Robin looked confused, as if she were realigning her memories and perceptions.

"They're good people, Robin. You don't pay back kindness like that by packing up and leaving town as soon as you're able to make a contribution."

"So you're staying to pay them back?" Comprehension dawned in her tone.

He slanted her an irritated look. "No. I'm not staying to pay them back. I'm staying because Forever is the kind of place I want to live. The kind of place where I want to raise my family. Sure, my business makes a contribution to the local economy, but it's no more than anyone else does."

"I know it's a good place, as far as small, isolated towns go, but there are so many other choices out there. Don't you ever wonder?"

He blew out a long sigh. She just wasn't getting this. Her with that see-the-world, to-hell-with-home, to-hell-with-him mentality. "I don't need other choices. I don't need a fast pace. I don't need the high life. It's a good town and I, for one, am standing by it."

"I see."

"No, I don't think you do." She'd unknowingly touched a nerve, and he sounded bitter without meaning to. "I'm grateful to this town. Not all of us want to bail for something bigger as soon as we get the chance."

She looked abruptly away. The wind ruffled her hair and her sigh blended with the ripple of the poplar leaves. "You must have a pretty low opinion of me."

He shook his head, dropping it forward. Why did he just do that? He'd always imagined he'd be worshiping at her feet if he was ever given another opportunity, and here he was denigrating her lifestyle with his holier-than-thou attitude.

He lifted his head. "I didn't mean—"

"Sure you did." She flipped back her hair. The flower dropped to the ground. "You think I'm ungrateful."

"I didn't say that."

"Just because I grew up here, doesn't mean you...*they* own me. Nobody owns me. Nobody has the right to keep me here."

The raw hurt he'd harbored for twenty-four hours—no, make that fifteen years—rushed to the surface. She'd left the town, left the people, left *him*, without a backward glance. She had done it without regret, without ever wondering what might have been.

"You've made that abundantly clear," he snapped. "I'm—*we're* not even a footnote in your life anymore."

She stared at him in injured silence. He knew he'd stepped way over the line with that crack.

He was a fool. It wasn't her fault the defining moment in his life hadn't been the defining moment in hers. It wasn't her fault he'd carried a torch all these years for a relationship that didn't even exist.

He reached out to touch her arm. "Robin—"

"You know nothing about me," she said.

He thought about her response in the Forever River, the way she clung to him, kissed him, begged him to make love to her. She'd been his. For one shining moment she'd been completely his. And he remembered every precious second.

"You're wrong about that," he replied. "I know everything that matters."

4

EVERYTHING THAT MATTERS? Robin gently lowered the bit from the mare's mouth, then walked the bridle into Jake's dim, well-ordered tack shed.

What did he mean by "everything that matters"? The muggy, oppressive prestorm air brought out the heavy scent of leather. It suited her mood. As did the gathering clouds.

He didn't know her at all. But for a frightening second, as she'd stared into his piercing eyes, she believed he could see right through to her soul.

Why had she been stupid enough to go riding with him? Had she thought they could erase fifteen years for a simple roll in the wildflowers? She should have realized that nothing about Jake had ever been simple.

He'd made her defensive. He'd made her feel guilty. In one fell swoop, he'd made her question beliefs and choices of a lifetime. For the sake of her own sanity, she needed to stay well away from him.

His boot heels thumped on the wooden floor behind her.

"Are we going to talk about it?" he asked.

"Talk about what?" She turned and started toward

the door, intending to brush past him and head home. There was no need to rehash the whole argument. He was small-town, she was big-world. End of story then, end of story now.

He took a half step sideways, blocking her way. "The elephant."

She tipped her chin to look at his face. The last African animal she remembered discussing was a lion. "What elephant?"

"It's a metaphor for that great big thing we're both ignoring. There's an elephant in the living room, Robin."

"I don't know what you're talking about," she said. But she very much feared she did.

"You can't tell me you don't remember." He inched closer. Daylight shone through the window, highlighting the planes and angles of his face. The scent of leather oil wafted around them.

She swallowed, taking a step back.

He stepped forward again. "Because I remember every second. I remember the way you looked. The way you felt. The sound of your voice. The taste of your—"

"Jake." Her voice trembled.

"Yeah?"

"Stop."

"Why?"

"I'm mad at you." What she really meant was *I'm scared of you.* She was scared of herself. She was scared of them. She was terrified of the cataclysmic power that quivered whenever they were together.

"I know. But that doesn't change the fact that we nearly made love fifteen years ago."

"I remember." She remembered with every fiber of her being.

"Damn straight." His gaze shifted to her lips.

Once again she saw longing turn to determination and then to resolve. Panic sizzled up her spine. She knew instinctively that if he kissed her, whatever fate had in mind fifteen years ago would be signed, sealed, and delivered right here on his tack room floor.

"I never thanked you," she interrupted.

"Thanked me?" He hesitated.

"You were a hero and a gentleman that night, and I never thanked you. So, uh, thank you."

He studied her expression, eyes narrowing. "Do you *want* me to kiss you?"

"No." The single word took every ounce of her willpower.

He stepped back. "Do you want some iced tea?"

"Huh?"

"Iced tea?" He moved away, turning toward the door. "I'm offering you a drink. You must be thirsty after the long ride."

Robin struggled to get her bearings. That was it? Just like that? She said no and he backed off?

She knew it was the politically correct thing to do and all. But he must not have been that crazy about kissing her in the first place. She started to feel insulted, but then realized she was being totally irrational.

She'd said no. She'd meant no.

"Sure," she said, resolving to be proud of herself and grateful to him all over again. "Iced tea sounds good."

THE INSIDE OF HIS HOUSE was magnificent. Robin paused in the doorway of a gourmet kitchen and gazed at the huge, polished-log dining room. It had a dozen floor-to-ceiling windows that overlooked the river. The table, which could easily seat twelve, was sculpted out of red-hued wood, inlaid with an exquisite contrasting blond grain that formed a swirling pattern around the edge. A matching sideboard lined one wall.

"Is it cherry?" she asked, taking a step forward to run a gentle finger along the curved edge.

"Yukon russet birch. Locally crafted."

"Really? It's wonderful." She was very impressed.

"Thank you. I don't like to brag, but I purchased it myself."

"Cute." She smiled and stepped back to admire the chairs. As long as she stayed a few feet away from Jake, this platonic truce seemed to be working.

He headed back into the kitchen. "I try to support Sullivan whenever I can."

"Sullivan?" She followed.

"Sullivan Creations." He took a pitcher of iced tea

out of the refrigerator. "The furniture company. Have you been away that long?"

"I knew somebody was using the russet birch trees, but I never imagined anything like this."

"Derek's done very well in the European market." He handed her a tall glass. "Do you mind if we drink in here?" He gestured to the breakfast bar.

"Of course not."

"I stayed up the mountain too long." He didn't say, *Fighting with you.* And, for that, Robin was grateful. She hadn't known him well in school, but she was beginning to like the man he'd become.

"Derek and his dinner guests are going to be here in an hour," said Jake.

"Derek brings his guests to your house for dinner?"

"All the time." He opened the steel-sided refrigerator and pulled out a plump chicken. "I was going to roast this, but I don't think we want to eat quite that late."

"Why doesn't Derek feed them himself? Or maybe take them to a restaurant?"

"The Fireweed Café?" Jake pasted her with a pained expression. "They're potential buyers from Europe."

"The meatloaf special won't do it?"

"And they don't like their wine on tap." He placed his hands on his hips as he contemplated the bird.

"What did you plan to serve?" She gathered her

hair up with one hand and tucked it into the back of her shirt.

"Roast chicken and shrimp cocktail."

She unbuttoned her cuffs and rolled up her sleeves. "Got a sharp knife?"

He glanced at her forearm. "I know we're running late, but I think suicide's a bit drastic."

She smiled and rolled her eyes. Oh, yeah, she liked him, all right. The trick was going to be in finding just the right balance of *liking*. "I was going to debone the chicken." She gestured to his refrigerator. "May I?"

"Be my guest."

She opened the door, plans beginning to form in her mind. They couldn't very well let the buyers starve. "You have any milk or cream?"

"Both." He peeked over her shoulder, placing a hand on the open door.

"Some kind of cheese? Feta? Blue? Emmental?" She spotted some fresh mushrooms and tomatoes and pulled them out of the drawer. Not a bad start.

"I have Feta. Why?"

"Wine?" She discovered lettuce and cucumbers. Even more possibilities opened up.

"My wine cellar is at your disposal. What are you doing?"

"We can make chicken Fricante with a seafood hollandaise sauce—you said you have lemons, right?"

"Chicken Fricante?"

"Yeah. And a marinated vegetable salad. Stuffed mushrooms. You wouldn't happen to have some of that smoked salmon that Mr. Brewster gives away every year, would you?"

"In my freezer."

"Perfect." She smiled, rubbing her hands together. "We're away to the races."

"How do you know all this?"

"Wild Ones sends all their guides to a Cordon Bleu course. I tagged along."

"You're kidding."

"Why do you keep saying that? I have a diploma to prove it. Fifty hours of instruction with Chef Henri. Though I must admit, we focused mainly on open campfires. But your stove will do in a pinch."

"It's propane," he said with a hopeful smile.

"Close enough."

He took a step back. "My kitchen is all yours. Just tell me how I can help."

She opened a couple of drawers before spotting a wooden knife block containing an assortment of knives on the counter. With a calculating smile, she withdrew a large carving knife. "Find me a pot. A big one. And any kind of pasta you happen to have on hand. Linguini would be nice."

"Yes, ma'am." He glanced down at the knife, an outrageously wary expression on his face. "Whatever you say, ma'am."

"So these people are from Europe?" she called as he disappeared into the pantry.

"Holland and France." He returned with a large box of spaghetti noodles. "These do?"

"Just fine."

"Derek has somebody over about once a month. He goes over to Europe quite often, too."

"So, why does he live..." She snapped her mouth shut. "Forget I asked that." She made a neat cut through the body cavity of the chicken to remove the back. "Can you boil me some water?"

"Absolutely. Derek is going to be so impressed."

"So, tell me again why they're coming here."

Jake lit a gas burner on the stove. "To see the factory."

"No. I mean, why your house?"

"I have a big dining room and a fairly extensive collection of Sullivan pieces. Derek gives me a discount and, in return, I play host."

"That's very generous of you."

"I have to do something with all this space."

TOGETHER THEY CHOPPED the vegetables, sliced the smoked salmon, shelled the shrimp and stuffed the mushroom caps. Fifteen minutes before the guests were due, Jake headed upstairs for a shower and Robin began to set the table. His china was exquisite, and she wondered just how much money he made raising bucking horses.

When the doorbell rang, she hesitated. The shower had stopped running only minutes before. She glanced down at her clothes, then pulled her hair out of the back of her shirt and ran her fingers quickly through it. It looked as though it would either be her in horse-worn clothing or Jake naked.

She quickly checked the annoyingly detailed image that thought created. Friends, she said to herself. She and Jake were going to be friends—polite, safe, friends. She headed for the front door.

"Hi, Robin." Derek betrayed absolutely no surprise at seeing her there.

"Hi." Her smile encompassed all five guests. The two people who'd watched the rodeo that afternoon stood on the deck, along with another couple who looked to be in their mid-fifties. The rain hadn't started yet, but the wind was picking up. Evening storms were common in August.

"Hi, Derek." Jake's voice on the stairs made her sigh with relief. "Come in, everyone."

Robin stepped back out of Jake's way.

Once they were all through the door, Derek made introductions. "Jeanette and Gerard Beauchamp, this is Robin Medford. And you've met Jake." The Beauchamps smiled in acknowledgment.

Derek turned to the other couple. "Jack and Nannie van der Pol, this is Jake Bronson and Robin Medford."

"Hello," the gentleman offered with a heavy Dutch accent. The woman smiled shyly.

"It'll be an interesting evening," Derek continued. "The Beauchamps speak French, very little English. And the van der Pols speak Dutch, also limited English."

Robin smiled at Nannie van der Pol. *"Zo Mevrouw van der Pol. Hoe vond u de zeis naar Whitehorse?"*

"Heel mooi boon. Zulke prachtige uitsidchten. Oh—U spreecht Hollands. Wat leuh!" Nannie grinned in delight.

"You speak *Dutch*?" Jake drew back in surprise.

Derek beamed.

Robin turned to the Beauchamps, figuring Jake's was a rhetorical question. *"Comment avez-vous aimé le 'rodéo' cet après-midi?"*

"C'était très excitant! Vous parlez très bien le français, mademoiselle."

"Merci. Je n'ai pas souvent l'occasion de le pratiquer."

"*French*, too?" Jake sounded as though one of the stuffed mushrooms had stuck in his throat.

"You are joining us for dinner, aren't you, Robin?" Derek asked hopefully.

She glanced up at Jake. "I wasn't planning—"

"Just a moment." Jake smiled at the guests then gently pulled her aside. "We need you!" he whispered frantically.

She frowned at him. "I can't eat dinner dressed like this. I smell like a horse."

"Go take a shower."

"I don't have time to go next door and still make the sauce," she hissed. "You want to ruin all our efforts by letting the chicken dry out?" Honest to God, gourmet kitchen and fine china aside, the man was a culinary Bohemian.

"Then shower upstairs." He turned his head and smiled reassuringly at the guests.

Robin blinked. Shower upstairs? As in *his* upstairs? *His* shower? Simple friends didn't inhale each other's steam.

"And change into *what?*" she protested, inching toward the back door.

"Raid my closet. I don't care what you look like."

"Jake." She tried a warning tone. This was not a good plan. On so many levels, this was *not* a good plan.

"Robin." He didn't look as if he was in the mood for a debate.

She tried to stare him down.

"Please?" His entreaty won her over. "I'll call home for you."

RAID HIS CLOSET. Raid his closet? What on earth was she going to find in here that she could possibly wear to dinner? She frantically shifted a group of hangers to the left.

Suits. He had very large suits and dress shirts that would look like tents on her. She shook her head in disgust. She figured she had about three minutes to come up with an outfit and dash through his shower before the chicken turned into leather.

She opened his top drawer. Boxer shorts and white T-shirts, now that would look interesting. Oh, and silk—wait a minute, black silk stockings? Upon closer inspection, she realized they were men's silk long johns.

She held them up to her waist. A bit large, but definitely better than the suit pants. Back in the closet, she grabbed a freshly pressed white dress shirt. In another drawer she found a collection of silk handkerchiefs, which she swiftly braided into a colorful belt. Along with her jewelry, it would have to do.

She headed for the shower, stripping her clothes off as she crossed the floor. Fortunately, there was no time to dwell on the intimacy of stepping into Jake's damp shower, or of borrowing his body soap, or viewing the personal toiletries that sat on the huge marble counter.

The man certainly had a great house.

JAKE SNAPPED his jaw shut as Robin drifted down the staircase. His clothes sure never looked that good on him.

His silk long underwear peeked out from between the tails of his shirt, flowing delicately against her thighs with every step. He had no idea where the colored belt had come from, but it accented her slender waist, giving a feminine shape to the boxy clothes. She was enchanting.

Standing next to the masterpiece she'd made of his table, smelling the gourmet dinner, and watching her bright smile as she descended into the room, he had to choke back the words, "Will you marry me?"

Stop! His hand tightened on the highball glass.

She'd said no to his kiss. He was pretty sure that did not bode well for a marriage proposal.

"I guess you won't be needing the letters anymore." Derek glanced from Jake to Robin, then back again.

"Letters?" asked Jake, reminding himself that she was leaving town in the next few days. There was only one way for her visit to end. Jake simply had to decide how badly his heart got broken.

"The personal ad answers," said Derek. "You've got *she's the one* stamped all over your goofy face."

Jake blinked. "Ain't happening," he said to Derek.

"The hell it's not. You should see your expression."

"She's leaving on Monday."

"That gives you four days."

Yeah. Right. Four days to set himself up for unimaginable heartache. He could *not* get involved with Robin. "I'm keeping the letters."

Derek chuckled. "Then maybe you should open one. But if you're keeping the letters, mind if I take a shot at keeping her here?" Derek's gaze slid appreciatively down the length of Robin's body.

"Don't touch her." Territorial rage erupted like a thunderhead within Jake, and he glared at Derek.

"Down, boy," said Derek. "I'm just yanking your chain." His expression turned serious. "If you don't take your best shot, you're going to kick yourself for the rest of your life. She looks good in your house, good in your clothes. I think you know she'd look good on you."

Jake took a healthy swallow of his single malt. Derek was not helping.

"Glass of wine, Robin?" Derek took advantage of a pause in the guests' conversation.

"Sure." She smiled warmly at Jake.

He smiled back and wondered exactly how much he could get away with before he was *involved*, technically speaking. Smiling was okay. Talking was good. Kissing was out—well, kissing on the mouth, anyway. Maybe he could kiss her somewhere else.

While Derek poured a glass of wine, she sat and spoke to the Beauchamps then to the van der Pols, switching smoothly from one language to the other. Both couples laughed.

THROUGHOUT the delicious meal, she helped him serve, she smiled, and she charmed, translating as if she were a diplomat at the United Nations. Jake carried on a halfhearted conversation with Derek, but mostly he just listened to the sound of Robin's voice. He liked French the best, he decided. The throaty cadences suited her.

When dinner was over, Derek asked Robin to join them on the factory tour the next day. Her translating services would be ideal. Jake wasn't too thrilled at the thought of Derek with Robin, but he could hardly protest.

When they finally closed the front door after the departing guests, she leaned against it and smiled. "Well, that was fun."

"Your brain must be tired." He boldly brushed a

curl off her forehead. It wasn't a kiss. It was only the slightest of touches. Beside, he'd been watching that curl for hours.

"Not too bad." She straightened and headed for the table. "Though a couple of times there I almost did a literal translation of a colloquialism. That would have been interesting."

Lightning seemed to punctuate her words, and thunder finally crackled overhead as she picked up a couple of wineglasses and headed for the kitchen.

"You don't have to do that." He gathered up the remainder of the glasses and followed her.

"I don't mind." She opened the nearly full dishwasher and laid the crystal carefully in the grooves of the top rack.

"Where did you learn Dutch, anyway?" He made no further protest about her cleaning efforts. If she wanted to hang around here and pick up wineglasses all night long, it was okay by him. He was certainly in no hurry to send her home.

"Wild Ones again. It's always easier to get around if you know the local language. They strongly support night-school language training." She stepped aside so he could set his glasses in the last two spaces on the rack.

"You do amazingly well for somebody who's just taken a few night-school classes." He closed the door of the dishwasher and pressed the On button. The quiet hum of the motor filled the room.

"I also get a chance to practice most of them with

fluent speakers." She headed back into the dining room. "That makes it a whole lot easier."

Jake followed. Robin had always been top of the class in high school. But there must be a level above genius he didn't even know about. No wonder Forever was too tame for her.

She plucked the used candles from the holders and set them aside.

"Exactly how many languages do you speak?" he asked.

She paused, a porcelain candle holder in each hand. "Including Latin?"

"What do you mean, *including* Latin?"

"Well, it's not a very practical language. I only took it because I had Thursdays free." She paused. "I mean, the chances of Derek arriving at the doorstep with somebody who knows nothing but Latin are pretty remote."

He stared at her stupidly.

She blinked a little uncertainly. "Don't you think?"

The woman spoke Latin. Nobody actually spoke Latin anymore. He knew a few colorful phrases, mostly from the front of fraternity T-shirts, but to actually carry on a conversation? He decided he didn't really want to know how many languages she spoke. It was too disheartening.

She frowned at the candlesticks. "Where did I get these from?"

"The drawer in the sideboard," he answered.

She opened the wide center drawer.

"No," he corrected, quickly coming around beside her. "Not that one, over—"

"What are these?" She set the candlesticks down and picked up one of the unopened envelopes. "'Yukon Jake'? Are you 'Yukon Jake'?" She looked at him quizzically. "They're from all over the country."

"Yeah." He cringed. "One end to the other."

"Do these people all want bucking horses?" She flipped the envelope over.

"Not exactly."

"Is it none of my business?" She quickly dropped the letter back in the drawer, a contrite expression on her face. "Sorry."

Good grief, she was going to think he was involved in something illegal or immoral. He sighed, closed his eyes and shook his head. He supposed telling her about Derek's ad would ensure he didn't start having hopeless fantasies about her. That was a plus.

"They're answers to a personal ad."

"For..." Her eyebrows lifted, and a sly grin formed on her face. "Do you have a secret life?"

"Nothing like that." Well, actually, it was something like that. But not that tacky.

"I'm sorry, Jake. You don't have to tell me anything."

"It's for a wife." He sighed.

Her eyes widened in shock. Her tone turned incredulous. "You took out a personal ad to find a wife?"

"No," he hastily assured her. "Well, Derek did. But he put my name on it. We were joking about it one night, and well..."

"Who wants the wife? You or Derek?" She placed a hand lightly on his forearm. "We can stop having this conversation whenever you want."

"You might as well know." He tried to ignore her warm hand. It was impossible. "The rest of the town does. Both of us want wives. He thought the personal ad was a good idea, and tested the waters using my name."

"Nice guy."

"That's what I said. Well, not exactly in those words." He wasn't about to repeat the phrase he'd used on Derek.

She moved her hand, and went back to the letters. "So, did you find somebody? Are you getting married?"

He searched her expression, trying to decide if she cared one way or the other. "I haven't opened any of the letters."

"Really?" Her Forever River eyes lit up. That pretty blue-green shimmered with interest and excitement. "Could we?" She gestured to the pile of letters with an eager grin, then let the question trail off.

Screen potential wives with Robin?

"I could help you pick one." She didn't need to look so eager to help. He wouldn't be the least bit thrilled to pick out a husband for her.

She waited for his answer.

Screening potential wives with Robin. It would certainly be a new highlight in the most bizarre moments of his life.

5

WHAT BETTER WAY to diffuse her increasing attraction to Jake? She'd help him find a wife. Then, no matter what kind of insane ideas she had about spending more time with him, even if fate gave her some crazy notion that she loved him, he'd be taken, unavailable, out of the running. It was perfect.

"What did the ad say?" she asked as they spread the letters out between them on the couch. The light was soft against the wooden walls, the storm rain spattered the black windowpanes.

He gave her a sly smile. "'Single white male seeks—'"

"No way." She laughed. Thunder rumbled in the distance.

"It said something about me wanting to meet an intelligent, outdoor-loving woman willing to relocate to a small northern town, with an eye to matrimony."

"Looks like there are quite a few willing outdoor women out there." There had to be fifty letters in the pile. She slit open the first one. "Oh, look. They sent a picture."

It was a very attractive woman, posing in shorts and a halter top beside a lake.

Jake lifted the glossy photograph from Robin's fingers. "Do you suppose that's really her?"

"Of course it's her. Why would she send a picture of somebody else?" Robin began reading the letter. "It says here she's thirty-four."

"That's a little old."

Robin frowned pointedly. "Watch it, buddy. *We're* thirty-two. It says she likes the outdoors, picnics, barbecues. Has a poodle." Robin read the next paragraph and couldn't hold back a giggle.

"What?"

"She's willing to relocate up north." Robin glanced at Jake over the top of the page. "Says she loves North Bay."

Jake rolled his eyes. "Oh, yeah, tiny, isolated North Bay, a whole three hours from downtown Toronto. Next."

"Should we start a *no* pile?"

"How about in the woodstove? No, wait, Derek wants to see the overflow. Save that one."

Robin set the letter on the coffee table and slit open the next envelope. Jake seemed content to lounge at the other end of the couch and let her read.

"Another picture. Hey, this one looks just like Cindy Crawford." She leaned forward to hand it to him.

"That *is* Cindy Crawford."

Robin grinned. "Cindy Crawford wants to marry you? You'd better scoop her up before she changes her mind."

Jake shook his head, tossing the picture onto the coffee table. "Next."

Robin focused on the next envelope, working her way into it with the opener. "This seems a bit drastic. Isn't there someone in town you'd like to marry?"

He didn't answer. His searing gaze penetrated her skin as the grandfather clock in the corner ticked off the seconds. "Not usually."

Robin wasn't touching that one.

No way.

No how.

No chance.

She didn't even glance up. "This looks good," she singsonged, scanning the next letter. "Twenty-seven years old. No picture, but she says she likes hiking and camping." Robin needed to marry this guy off before she started getting any crazy ideas.

"Where's she from?" he asked.

"Vancouver. Oh. Do you like snakes?"

"I don't want to hear this."

"She has a breeding pair of pythons."

Jake groaned.

Robin laughed. "She say's they're very gentle with children."

"Not my children. Next."

"Don't worry, Jake. There are at least forty letters left." She opened another. "We'll find somebody for you."

"I'm sending the snake lady to Derek. You want coffee or something?"

"Sure. Oh. My."

"What?"

"Do you think this one's a transvestite?" Robin held up the picture so Jake could see it.

"Holy cow. I'd be scared to procreate. Derek definitely gets that one." He stood. "How do you take your coffee?"

"Black. Maybe you should take a trip to Vancouver or Edmonton and try to meet somebody." Robin abandoned the letters and followed Jake into the dimly lit kitchen. There didn't seem to be a lot of normal people answering personal ads these days.

"Tried that. Several times, as a matter of fact."

"I don't understand. You're an intelligent, good-looking guy—"

"Why, thank you." He peeled the plastic lid off a coffee can.

"If you're serious about this, I think you're unnecessarily handicapping yourself. You could raise horses anywhere."

Jake's jaw tightened. He very deliberately set down the coffee can. A streak of lightning whitened the room, highlighting his stone-sculpted features. Thunder followed on its heels.

She swallowed, but pressed on. "Have you considered moving to a bigger center?"

He pasted her with a granite stare. "Yes. I've considered it."

"And?" She shivered under his scrutiny.

"I'd resent the woman who made me leave." He

shook his head and began scooping coffee into the filter basket.

"Oh." She ran her fingertip along his smooth countertop.

He gently closed the plastic top on the coffeemaker, and his voice took on a softer teasing quality. "So, what about you? You're an intelligent good-looking woman..."

She grinned and rolled her eyes, grateful for his change in mood. "Why, thank you."

"Why aren't you married?"

"I've been from Argentina to Zimbabwe. Never met the right man."

"Ever think about broadening your options?"

Lightning and thunder cracked simultaneously, making her jump. "What do you mean?"

"Ever think of moving back to Forever?"

She stared at Jake while the storm battered the atmosphere around them. The longing to reach for him, to touch him, to hold him in her arms, was almost overpowering. But he was suddenly a perilous threat to her freedom.

Her heart contracted in her chest, and the coffee sizzled into the bottom of the carafe. She licked her dry lips. "I'd end up resenting the man who made me stay."

JAKE WAS NOT GOING to make her stay. No matter what his charcoal-blue eyes promised. No matter how forlorn he looked or how forlorn she felt when they tiptoed around their emotions. She wasn't compromising on this. Staying in Forever was worse than unthinkable.

She straightened the quilt that was draped over top of her.

She was strong. She was focused. Five days in this town was not going to undo a lifetime of planning and hard work—no matter how good-looking and intelligent the man. As she'd told Connie, it was *not* the 1950s. Women did *not* define their lives based on a husband.

She pulled the basal body thermometer out of her mouth. She had a fertility plan. She had a new job in Toronto. She had nannies and preschools all lined up. She had a *life* out there.

Rolling over on the bed, she held the thermometer to the window to read the scale in the morning sunshine. She blinked at the temperature reading. Rubbed her eyes, then checked it again.

Well, that was unexpected.

It was up. According to the thermometer, she could get pregnant anytime in the next three days.

If she wanted to.

If she had the right man around.

If, say, there was somebody here in Forever who was good-looking and intelligent. Who would make a good father. Who wouldn't mind...

She swallowed.

Could she make love with Jake and escape unscathed? Now there was a perilous thought. She bit down on her thumbnail.

He'd be the perfect candidate. She couldn't ask for a better genetic specimen.

Maybe if she focused on the goal line.

Maybe if she protected her emotions.

Maybe if, as Connie said, she went after what she wanted like a steamroller, neither looking to the left nor the right. Maybe she could do it.

If she could, she'd have a little Jake running around. This time next year, she'd have a little dark-haired, blue-eyed boy or girl in her arms.

The thought made her warm with longing. Her hand trailed across her abdomen. She wondered how it would look, rounded with a baby. Not just any baby. Now that she'd pictured Jake's child, she couldn't imagine having one with anyone else.

"HI, MOM. Hi, Connie." Robin padded barefoot into the kitchen, heading straight for the aromatic coffee-pot. She struggled to contain a strange mixture of anxiety and anticipation bubbling inside her.

"You sound chipper this morning." Dressed in a cozy burgundy robe, her mother, Eunice, was frying bacon at the stove. The kitchen was just as Robin remembered it as a child. She couldn't count the number of times she'd come downstairs on a lazy Saturday morning to her mother and grandmother making breakfast.

Connie remembered their father, but he'd died

when Robin was only three and was only a hazy shadow to her. Her grandmother, mother and Connie were her family.

"It's a beautiful day." She took a deep breath and smiled, pouring herself a generous mug of coffee. It was fun to be back for a little while.

"You were late getting home last night," said Connie as she flipped a row of pancakes. "We thought you'd sleep in."

Sleep? Sleep was definitely not on the agenda for this morning. She was fertile. The opportunities were endless. "Did Jake tell you I was helping Derek translate?"

"He did," answered Connie.

"It's nice to see you so cheerful." Grandma patted Robin's arm as Robin sat next to her at the table.

"Good morning, Grandma." Robin leaned over to kiss her papery cheek. "How are you feeling?"

"Right as rain," said Grandma, turning the page of a large-print novel. "Connie's boys are taking me for a walk to see the swans this morning. That Sammy is the spitting image of his great-grandfather, don't you think? Eunice, did you find my wool sweater?"

"Found it, Mom."

"Don't tell the boys Grandma's already seen the swans," Connie cautioned. "They're about beside themselves thinking they'll surprise her."

Grandma chuckled. "They think because I'm old, I haven't noticed those birds flying over for three days."

"Won't say a word," Robin promised.

"How's their wife hunt going?" asked Connie.

"Uh, not too well," Robin replied.

"They should have come to us. We could have helped," said Eunice with a wave of her flipper.

Welcome back to your small town. Robin took a sip of the scalding coffee. No secrets here.

"Have you met Derek?" asked Grandma. "He's a nice boy."

"I met him last night," said Robin.

"He's a nice boy. Owns his own company, you know."

"I know, Grandma."

"Good-looking, too."

"I'm not marrying Derek, Grandma." Robin grinned.

"The boy's got money."

"Sorry, Grandma."

"Oh, well. An old lady can hope, can't she?"

"I'm not getting married. I'm starting a new job on Monday. But he did ask me to help him translate at a mill tour this afternoon."

"You take a good long look at that boy before you make up your mind." Grandma waggled a finger. "You know I still manage a wee bit of Estonian now and then."

"This is Dutch and French," said Robin. "Or I'd

bring you along. I must get my knack for languages from you."

"Wouldn't surprise me," said Eunice. "I always got straight A's in French. Must be an inherited trait on the maternal side."

"Well, I was hopeless in French *and* Athapaskan," said Connie as she put a platter of pancakes into the oven. "Robin got the language gene."

"But you ended up with that great motherhood gene." Eunice affectionately squeezed the shoulders of her oldest daughter. "We're grateful to you every day of the year for giving us those beautiful grandchildren."

Connie glanced at Robin and gave her a conspiratorial look, acknowledging the fact that more beautiful grandchildren might yet make their mother and grandmother grateful.

Robin smiled back. She experienced the anxiety and anticipation she'd felt a few moments ago. Connie had no idea just how soon that might happen.

There was a scream from the living room. "Mom! Sammy hit me."

"Care to reconsider that gratitude, Mom?" Connie shook her head and scooped out another measure of batter.

"He's just a little exuberant," said Eunice. "Be patient with him. Sometimes the things that drive you crazy in small boys, you absolutely love in men."

Bobbie shot into the room and launched himself

onto Robin's lap. "Save me, Auntie Robin." He wrapped his arms tightly around her neck.

"He threw his truck at me," Sammy protested, sliding to a halt in front of Robin.

"Did you throw your truck?" Robin whispered in Bobby's ear. She enjoyed the warmth of his little body.

"Not hard," said Bobby.

"See," said Sammy.

"Pancakes before we go to the river?" asked Connie.

The argument was immediately forgotten.

THE BIRTHDAY PARTY was Saturday, but Jake had offered up his house on Thursday night so everybody could get together to make the final plans. About twenty of the townspeople were coming over to discuss everything from setting up the huge festival tent in the park to music, decorating and refreshments. Since virtually the entire town was invited to the dinner and dance, the big tent was the only space large enough.

As Jake took a final glance around his neat, empty house, he couldn't help remembering how much fun he'd had last night when Robin was around to help him get ready for company. Now the place sort of echoed.

The doorbell rang. Shaking off the feeling, he headed to answer it.

WITHIN HALF AN HOUR the living room and dining room were packed with people. When Robin finally arrived with her mother and Connie, Jake instinctively moved toward her.

Annie Miller beat him to it.

"You look gorgeous." Annie enfolded Robin in a long, warm hug. Jealousy trickled through Jake.

Robin frowned down at her dress. "I only expected to need one formal outfit. I had to pull my grad dress out of the attic."

It was the same little formfitting spaghetti-strapped number she'd driven Jake crazy with fifteen years ago. If she'd planned to send him over the edge tonight, she couldn't have succeeded better.

"It fits?" Annie rolled her eyes. "I hate you."

Robin stepped back to admire Annie. "You look absolutely stunning."

Annie looked just fine, but it was Robin that sent his pulse off the charts. Jake moved toward them. "Would you ladies like some wine?"

Annie nodded with a wide smile.

"Sounds good," said Robin. "Want some help?"

"I'll give you a hand." Derek's voice interrupted Jake's answer. Jake pasted a smile on his face and thanked Derek. Robin was the one he wanted to get alone in the wine cellar. Not Derek.

JAKE CAUGHT no more than glimpses of Robin for most of the evening as he hosted and helped strategize the tent erecting for the next day. Robin was co-opted to the decorating committee, and she spent most of the night laughing and chatting with Annie and Connie.

As the women talked, Robin's contemplative gaze kept straying to Derek. Though Derek's threat to romance Robin had been made in jest, jealousy gnawed at Jake's gut. He gritted his teeth and forced himself to focus on the men at the table.

The tent framework was complicated. Patrick Moore was the resident expert, having overseen every tent erection since the town had purchased it five years ago. He was handing out work assignments as though he were a sergeant major.

"Jake?" Robin's whispered voice next to his ear sent his blood pressure soaring.

"Yeah?" He tipped his chair back from the table.

"Do you think we could dance tonight?"

"Sure." Anytime, anywhere, anyhow.

"The thing is..." She glanced around nervously, then motioned him away from the table with a little toss of her head.

He happily followed her to a corner of the dining room. This was more like it. Robin's attention should be on him not on Derek.

"The thing is, I think Annie's interested in Derek."

"What makes you say that?"

"We were talking, and...well...I just think she is. Okay?"

"Sure." It was fine with him. Just so long as Robin wasn't interested in Derek.

In fact, they could forget about Annie and Derek altogether. Jake wanted to get back to the dancing discussion. Him and Robin. He wanted to hold that classic little black dress against his body and pretend he'd died and gone to heaven.

"I thought..." she continued. "I thought if you put on some music, maybe we could get them to dance together."

"Why are you matchmaking Annie and Derek?" He breathed in her perfume. He liked it better when her attention was on him. Self-centered, he knew, but there it was.

She raised her eyebrows and gave him an exasperated look. "Derek's looking for a wife. I think Annie's interested, but she won't do anything about it because she works for him."

"I thought you were finding *me* a wife." One spaghetti strap had worked its way to the edge of her shoulder. He was itching to put it back. Or better still, pull it over the edge and taste her smooth, tanned skin once more.

"Are *you* interested in Annie?" she asked.

"No! No."

"Then let's help Derek. What kind of a friend are you? You were willing to give him Snake Woman, but you won't help him get Annie?" Mock indignation rose in Robin's eyes.

Jake chuckled. "He and Annie have worked together for five years. Don't you think if something was going to happen it would have happened by now?"

"Just put on some music." She smiled and blinked her long lashes. "Please?"

"Sure. No problem." She wanted music. He'd make music.

"And get Derek to ask her to dance."

"Give a woman an inch..." he deadpanned.

"Thanks, Jake." She patted his shoulder. "You're a pal."

A pal? Jake headed for the stereo system. Derek got dance music and a pretty woman in his arms. Jake got to be a pal. Wasn't that just swell.

Most of the committees were finished planning, so a group of men helped Jake move the dining-room table to open up the hardwood floor. He turned on some waltz music then headed for Derek.

Forever citizens didn't need a second invitation to dance, so the dining-room floor filled quickly.

"Dancing?" asked Derek as Jake came to a stop.

"Some of the women asked." Jake finished his glass of Bordeaux and set it aside.

Derek nodded, watching the swirling bodies mingle on the dance floor.

"Did you see Annie tonight?" Jake felt like a fool trying to set Derek up. Maybe he should just pass him a note after study hall.

"Yeah. Doesn't she look great when she dresses up?"

"Sure does." This was going pretty well so far.

Connie and her husband danced by. "Why don't you ask her to dance?" Jake suggested.

"Connie? Robert would disembowel me if I danced with his wife." Robert had received his economics degree on a football scholarship, and was notoriously protective of Connie.

"No. I mean Annie."

"There are laws against that," said Derek in a tone that clearly questioned Jake's sanity.

"What are you talking about?" Jake shot his friend an incredulous look.

"She's my employee," Derek explained. "I'm sure it never comes up between you and your wranglers, but it's called sexual harassment."

"I was only suggesting you *dance* with her. There doesn't have to be any sex involved."

"Doesn't matter." Derek shook his head. "Ask any lawyer. Say I ask her to dance. Maybe she doesn't want to dance with me, but she says yes because she thinks she has to be nice to the boss."

"That's crazy."

"Nope. I've got economic power over her. If I make any kind of overture, she can sue my butt off."

"You're paranoid. I guarantee Annie's not going to sue you for asking her to dance."

"We're never going to find out."

Jake sighed in disgust. A few minutes later, mumbling an excuse, he left Derek to find Robin.

"No go," he whispered, using the music as an excuse to get up close as he spoke to her.

"What do you mean, no go?" She turned toward him and he could smell that wonderful perfume again.

He let his cheek brush her hair while ostensibly talking close to her ear. "Derek won't ask Annie to dance."

"Why not?"

He rested his arm against her shoulder. "He's her employer. He's afraid she'll think it's sexual harassment."

"That's crazy."

"That's what I said."

"Go ask him again."

"It's not going to work."

She bit her lower lip.

"Dance with me."

"You got it." He didn't hesitate, didn't ask why. He didn't ask anything, just swept her up into his arms and whirled her onto the dance floor.

"Jake?" Her stocking-covered legs whispered against his slacks. Her breasts brushed his rib cage, and he was instantly engulfed in his own personal heaven.

"Yeah?"

"Here's the plan." She sounded like a bumbling espionage agent from some B-grade movie.

"The *plan*?"

"You ask Annie to dance. I'll ask Derek."

Jake couldn't say that he liked the plan so far.

"Then we'll swap partners."

"Robin, you're getting a little carried away here. They're adults. Let them figure out their own lives."

"Come on, Jake. Sometimes fate needs a little push."

"I don't want to be fate." He just wanted to hold her in his arms for the rest of the night.

"You're *not* fate," she said, a funny catch to her voice.

"Okay. Okay. We can't very well set Derek up with Snake Woman and the transvestite. Let's do it."

"Thanks," she whispered with a brilliant smile.

IN THE END Annie and Derek danced together for three songs straight. Robin was elated.

As the party wound down, Annie joined her in the kitchen to help with the cleanup. Robin could hardly contain her curiosity.

"You danced with Derek?" She tried to sound casual as she replaced the dishwasher-warm stemware in Jake's cabinet.

"Mmm-hmm." Annie glided across the room.

"And?" Robin raised her eyebrows expectantly.

Annie collected a stack of plates from the dishwasher rack. "And what?"

"How was it?"

Annie laughed lightly. "He spent the first song explaining in excruciating detail that I wasn't obligated to dance with him. And that our social dancing had nothing whatsoever to do with our relationship at work. I think he might have quoted a law or two."

Robin grinned, rolling her eyes and shaking her head.

"By the second song, he relaxed a little. He's always been a nice boss. He's a good dancer, too."

"Did he ask you out or anything?"

Annie looked puzzled. "Like on a date?"

"Yeah."

"No. Why would he do that? It was just a dance." She closed the empty dishwasher.

"Oh." Robin squelched her disappointment. She didn't know what she'd hoped for. She supposed a proposal was a bit much to expect right off the bat. She and Jake would have to come up with another plan.

"You two about ready to call it a night?" Jake appeared in the dining-room doorway, tie loosened, hair slightly mussed. "The housekeeper will finish up in the morning."

"Has everyone gone?" Robin had held out the hope that Derek would drive Annie home.

"Everyone but Annie's mom. She's waiting for you in the car, Annie."

"Thanks for the party, Jake." Annie closed a cupboard door on her way by. "See you both at the tent raising tomorrow."

"'Bye," said Robin with a wave.

The front door banged shut. Matchmaking was over for the evening, and she and Jake were alone.

Anxiety overtook Robin in a rush. She busily straightened the last few items on the counter.

Seducing Jake to get herself pregnant had seemed a whole lot simpler and more straightforward when she'd planned it from the privacy of her bedroom. Now that he was standing here in front of her, she didn't know how to start. It was quite possible that he wouldn't even be interested.

She wasn't exactly anybody's idea of a hot babe at the moment. Her dress was a little worse for the dishwashing duty, and her hair was limp from the steam. Her makeup had long since faded.

When she looked at Jake, she didn't feel like a focused steamroller heading for procreation. She felt like a nervous, vulnerable woman who needed to be comforted. The space between them seemed insurmountable.

She wished she could go back to when they were dancing—back to where she could feel his strength and hear his voice from the safety of his arms. Maybe then she'd be bold enough to make a serious move.

"Thanks for helping," he said. "But you didn't have to cleanup."

She felt a rush of guilt. It wasn't exactly altruism that had kept her in the kitchen. She'd been stalling for time, hoping to get him alone for her own selfish purposes.

She swallowed. Her plan suddenly seemed rash and ridiculous. "I didn't mind," she assured him around dry vocal chords.

She couldn't do this.

But she *had* to do this.

It was either Jake here or some other man in Toronto. She sure couldn't get pregnant all by herself.

He whisked a dish towel off the counter and hung it on the rack beside her. "Well, it was a big help."

His smile was warm. Dare she say fond? Maybe he'd make the first move. She'd be okay if he made the first move. If he'd just lean down and kiss her the way he had fifteen years ago, she could let herself go on a wave of passion.

Unfortunately, there was more compassion than passion in his eyes. "Tired?"

She found herself responding to the compassion. Maybe this whole seduction thing could wait for tomorrow. She'd be stronger tomorrow. More focused. "A little. I'm sweaty and my dress got splashed with dishwater."

Well, that information was certainly a long way from seductive.

"You need a nice long soak in the tub."

She sighed in genuine pleasure at the thought. "In case you didn't notice, there are eight people staying at Mom's house. I won't get near the bathroom until about 3:00 a.m."

"Use my tub."

Use his tub?

Use his tub!

Now there was a seduction opportunity on a silver platter. "You wouldn't mind?"

"With all due respect to your mother's tub, mine has jets."

"Yeah?" Jets were good. Jets were sexy. Now if she could just figure out a way to get him to join her in his jetted tub, she'd be pregnant in no time.

"You go on up." He nodded toward the staircase. "I'll finish up down here."

And then? Was there an *and then* in that statement?

6

ROBIN was in his tub.

From the box of his pickup truck, Jake sent the twentieth bale of hay sailing through the open shed door. His head pounded and his muscles burned from the breakneck pace. But at least the physical exertion was keeping him from striding into the house, mounting the stairs and stripping off his clothes to join her.

Lightning flashed in the black sky above. Then thunder rumbled as the first fat drops of the evening's storm soaked into his dress shirt. He heaved the last bale into the shed, then leaped to the ground and stalked inside.

Not stopping to catch his breath, he started stacking bales against the back wall.

His muscles knotted against the weight, and the bale strings cut into his gloved hands. But not even the pain could banish the vivid memory of Robin dancing in his arms. He could still hear her soft voice while she plotted to match-make Derek and Annie. He could smell her perfume and feel her small hands gripping his shoulders.

He tossed the last bale up high on the stack. "Use

my tub," he mimicked his own voice in the hollow, cold building.

Brilliant idea. A perfect recipe for insanity. Take the woman of your dreams—the one who, incidentally, just said *no* to your kiss and made it abundantly clear that she wasn't sticking around town for romance or anything else—put her naked in your bedroom, then just see how long it takes before you go stark raving mad. A sudden deluge of rain rattled the shake roof.

Jake wiped his forehead with the back of his hand. He walked stiffly out of the shed, latching the door behind him. Closing his eyes, he raised his face to the sky. The icy raindrops felt good. He let them pour over his overheated emotions like a balm.

After a few long moments and many deep breaths, he shook his wet hair and started down the path to the back deck. The en suite was dark. Thank goodness. If he was lucky, she'd already gone home.

If he was unlucky, she was changing in his bedroom, and he'd have to go jump in the river.

He lengthened his stride, wondering if her perfume would linger in his towels. His gaze dropped from the en suite window to the kitchen deck, and his heart lodged in his throat.

Robin wasn't changing in his bedroom. And she had definitely *not* gone home.

She'd commandeered another one of his white dress shirts. She was bathed in the glow of the yard lights, his shirt plastered to her skin by the driving rain. The sexiest woman in the world was standing on his porch.

Waiting?

Wanting?

Did this mean she'd changed her mind about kissing him? He quickened his pace. This definitely meant she'd changed her mind.

Only a fool could be unaware that the shirt clung to her body like a second skin. Robin was not a fool. And she wasn't a woman hesitating over a simple kiss. She was a woman holding up a neon sign that said love me.

He clenched his fingers around the reinforced palms of his leather gloves. He cautioned himself about jumping to conclusions, but his heartbeat deepened with every step.

She was here in Forever. She was standing on his deck. She was wearing his clothes. And she didn't look as if she was going anywhere anytime soon.

He mounted the stairs two at a time. She turned slowly to meet him, eyes wide. Her wet hair was combed back from her temples, highlighting her creamy-smooth skin and elegant features.

"You're getting soaked," he said, amazed that his voice sounded anywhere near normal. He loosened the leather gloves one finger at a time, then deliberately placed them on the rail.

"So are you." The slight tremble of her mouth betrayed her uncertainty.

He sucked in a breath. His eyes strayed downward.

Wet cotton outlined her breasts, her belly, and the dark shadow at the apex of her thighs. She was naked underneath his shirt.

"You must be cold." Where he was burning up.

He liked her wet. But he also liked her warm.

"Let's get you back inside." He wrapped his fingers around her chilled hand and pulled her toward him. He could see the little green streaks that made her irises shimmer like the mobile river water. He loved those little green streaks.

His name on her lips was an invitation.

He wiped a raindrop from her face with the pad of his thumb. Her thick lashes fluttered downward.

"You're exquisite," he whispered. "You've always been so exquisite."

Her lips curved up in a small smile. "And you've always been a gentleman."

"I'm not a gentleman, Robin." He splayed a hand across the curve of her spine, boldly pulling her against his hardening body. If he was misreading her signals, he wanted to know about it right away.

"I'm just a man. A man who has wanted you his whole life."

She didn't hesitate, didn't back away.

It looked as though the signals were coming through loud and clear.

He leaned down to kiss her rain-chilled lips. He did so, gently at first, tentatively, still gauging her reaction. He wasn't quite ready to believe this was truly happening. Her lips were soft, responsive, and they quickly warmed beneath his own.

Encouraged, he opened wider, pressed harder. She followed his lead, her lips silently urging him on. She tasted of wine, dark and heady. He wrapped his arms around her, enfolding her in his embrace.

Memories slammed into his conscious mind, kick-starting a wave of desire that roared through his bloodstream. He broke the kiss, gasping for breath.

Then he swept her into his arms and strode across the deck, carrying her inside, slamming the door behind them.

THE RAINDROPS BATTED loudly against the glass, counterpoint to the galloping rhythm of his heart.

He lowered her bare feet to the floor, turning so that her back rested against his entry wall. He leaned down to kiss her swollen lips, struggling to hold back an intense groan of satisfaction as he flew back in time. She was wet and willing in his arms once again. Only this time he had no intention of being noble.

The lights were dim. The waning citrus candles blended with her shampoo. Make that his shampoo.

His soap.

His shirt.

His, his, his.

He buried his fingers in her hair, anchoring her to him. The tip of her tongue found his. He responded with a hot invasion. She moaned, her hands moving along his arms to his shoulders where she held on tight.

He shifted to cradle her rib cage, feeling her heartbeat, the soft swell of her breasts, and remembering—oh, sweet heaven, remembering...

A stampede of desire decimated his reasoning power as his every fantasy came alive in his arms. She was sweet and soft and incredible.

"Robin," he breathed between desperate kisses. "I want..." He wanted so much. He wanted all of her. He wanted everything. He wanted with a need so strong it terrified and humbled him.

He pulled back, settling her once again against the wall. She blinked, hypnotically. Her breathing was heavy, the pulse in her neck jumping out of control. Her breasts spiked pink against the wet fabric.

He groaned then, cupping the weight of one breast in his palm. Unable to hold back, he dipped his head to taste.

"This isn't what I..." she whimpered, fingers tangling in his hair, bare legs ensnarling with his covered ones.

"Oh, Jake, I never..." She gasped.

"Do you want me to stop?" He didn't know if he could. He truly didn't know if he had it in him to call another halt.

"No!" That was good. That was emphatic.

"Thank goodness." He caught her as her knees gave way, lifting her in his arms and striding for the bedroom.

IN JAKE'S DARKENED bedroom, Robin trembled. He cradled the back of her head, covering her lips in yet another mind-numbing kiss. Steamroller, she reminded herself, savoring the taste of him. His knee worked its way between her thighs, and her body instantly convulsed.

Focus.

She inhaled deeply, tasting both wine and memories. Liking his kisses was part of the plan, she told herself. She was fine. This was all right on track.

Goal line.

His tongue swept the inside of her mouth and every muscle in her body turned to jelly. If not for the bed behind her and Jake's arm supporting her, she would have melted to the floor.

But that was okay. His kisses were allowed to turn her on. And hers were supposed to turn him on. Judging by the heat from their mingled panting, the kisses were doing their job.

She tipped her head back. Passionate kisses led to passionate lovemaking.

With the pad of her index finger, she stroked his whisker-roughened chin. Passionate lovemaking led to beautiful babies.

Beautiful babies were the goal line.

He captured her finger, pulling it deep into his hot mouth. Desire rocketed through her. She had to remember the goal line. Little Jakes with charcoal-blue eyes and dark hair.

Focus.

Jake kissed her again, fumbling with the buttons on his shirt, his hand struggling to maneuver between their straining bodies. With a pithy curse, he grabbed a handful of fabric and ripped the shirt from his chest. Buttons scattered to the four corners of the room.

He shrugged out of it, never breaking their kiss. She flattened her hand against his bare chest, stroking upward, feeling the rough, sparse hair as she made her way to his shoulders. He was broader, harder, rougher than the boy of eighteen, but he was still fundamentally Jake.

His iron muscles flexed under her hands. And she was safe once again. Safe in Jake's arms, she hung on tight as the world fell away.

He fumbled with her buttons, giving up more easily this time, ruining yet another of his shirts as he forcibly separated the halves of the damp fabric, exposing her body. Then he held her away while his heated blue gaze took its sweet crackling time.

"You're amazing," he whispered. "All this time. All these years."

His words filled her senses.

"Do you have any idea how hard it was for me to walk away from you?" he asked.

Was it hard? He'd seemed so strong, so sure of himself. But it hadn't been easy for him, either. She was glad.

"You're everything I ever wanted." He cupped her chin and kissed her gently. His free hand grazed her stomach. It gently swirled its way up her rib cage, teasing the bottom of her bare breast.

Her body strained toward him. She wrapped her hands around his contoured biceps.

Goal line.

Focus.

She could do this. She wasn't falling in love. He was simply the best kisser on the planet. And they had a history. This moment had been fifteen years in the making, and it was only natural for it to feel larger than life.

His fingertips found her nipple. Her brain became a psychedelic haze of nerve receptors. She forgot the time, the place, the century. Everything that had once anchored her disappeared. His fingers and lips were all that kept her from free-falling into space.

With a mounting sense of urgency, she reached for the button at his waist. His breath hissed out as she lowered the zipper and felt the hard heat of him through his cotton briefs.

His leather-tough palms gripped the backs of her thighs, climbing higher and higher. The cold, wet shirt teased her overheated skin. Her legs went limp.

Slowly, gently, he laid her back on the bed. He kicked off his pants and followed her down. The hot weight of him pinned her against the mattress. His burgeoning flesh pressed intimately against her.

"You completely blow my mind," he said hoarsely.

Now, now, now, her body screamed. She shifted her hips beneath him.

He reached to one side. She heard a drawer open.

"What?" Her short question came out on a gasp.

"Protection."

Goal line. Steamroller. Focus. "No."

He straightened his arms, pushing up, looming above her. His eyes were flints, his jaw muscles tight enough to snap. "You're saying *no?*" his voice rasped in disbelief.

"No." She shook her head. "Not *no.*"

His lower body still pressed against her. All it would take was one movement, a single thrust.

"No condom." Her hips tilted reflexively, and he groaned her name.

"What are you talking about?" His breath came in short pants.

"You don't need it."

"Are you on the Pill?"

She paused.

He gritted his teeth, his words coming hard. "I don't know how long you can hover on the edge of oblivion here, but *I* need an answer."

"You don't need a condom."

"That's not what I asked."

He flipped her hair out of the way, baring her lie-detecting neck to his gaze. "Are you on the Pill?"

"No."

He paused. He gazed intently into her eyes. He glanced at her breasts, then lower to where their bodies met. His hips flexed almost imperceptibly.

He swore. "No. No. I can't do this. You're not on

the Pill, but you want unprotected sex? You have to explain."

"Later," she breathed, and reached down.

He grabbed her wrist in an iron grip.

"Now." His eyes darkened to pewter.

"I want a baby." She stilled, waiting for his reaction.

"*What?*" The single word burst from somewhere below his diaphragm—fast, hot, lethal. It rivaled the lightning outside the window.

"A baby," she repeated.

"*That's* what this is all about?" His eyes closed. The corded muscles in his neck bulged.

She nodded slowly. "Yes."

"My baby?"

"Your baby."

He emitted a single disgusted curse and flipped onto his back. She was instantly cold without him, and she pulled the edges of the damp shirt over her body.

He didn't speak, but she could hear his breath shudder in and out. "And just what were you planning to do with *my* baby?"

She didn't understand the question, but took a stab at it, anyway. "Raise it."

"Where?"

"Toronto."

"Not Forever."

"Not Forever."

He jackknifed into a sitting position, raking a hand

through his hair. The muscles on his back stood out like sculpted steel. "There are males standing at stud on this ranch, Robin." He spat the words out. "But I am *not* one of them."

"It's wasn't like—"

He twisted around to glare at her. "You wanted a stud. Let's not pretty it up."

"I didn't think you'd—"

"Jeez." He barked out a harsh, unfeeling laugh. "I get thousands of dollars for one of my stallions."

"You want money?" She couldn't believe she heard him right.

"Don't be obscene. I think you'd better leave."

"Jake." She tried to reason with him, reaching out to touch his arm.

He jerked away as if she'd stung him. "Leave."

"I think you're overreacting."

His nostrils flared, but he didn't answer.

She wanted his baby because she admired and respected him. If he'd quit knee-jerk reacting all over the place, she could explain what a great mother she could be.

"If you'll give me a chance—"

He shot up and stalked toward the door.

"Jake," she called.

He didn't acknowledge her. For goodness' sake, the man was practically sulking.

"I think you're overreacting," she repeated in a lower voice. "And I bet I can change your mind."

He froze, one hand jerked up to grip the doorjamb.

The light from the hallway cascaded over his naked body. With a last lingering look at her, curled across his quilt, he shook his head.

"Fly at it, babe," he said. And then he was gone.

IN RETROSPECT, "Fly at it, babe," was probably not the best parting shot in the world. When Jake thought about it dispassionately, he had to admit it pretty much sounded like a dare.

And now he was going to have to live with the consequences of that dare.

He was stuck on wrench duty at the festival tent frame where Robin kept wandering around through his line of sight. She was toying with him. With every pass, her breasts shifted enticingly under her T-shirt, making it impossible for him to concentrate on the blueprints.

He was certain she knew exactly what effect she was having on him. No more than forty feet away, she moved her arms up, down and sideways, pointing out imaginary decorations to Connie and Annie. Each position revealed a new angle of her anatomy through the thin T-shirt.

Sweat formed between his shoulder blades as he yanked on the crescent wrench. The wrench slipped and his wrist slammed into the steel girder. He cursed under his breath, forcing his gaze away from Robin.

She had an adorable dirt smudge on her cheek, too.

One that she'd probably put there on purpose. It was a nice even smudge.

Just enough that he'd want to rub off. Just enough to guarantee he'd be thinking about the texture of her skin all morning long in the heat of the sun.

He lifted another bolt from a pocket of his leather tool belt and spun it onto the steel frame. Yeah, he knew what she was up to, all right. Remote seduction.

He should have expected something like this. A woman who would seduce a man with no intention of having a long-term relationship, simply to get pregnant, was capable of anything.

He'd lain awake long into the night thinking about her, imagining he could still smell her scent in his bed. He'd alternately beat himself up for having been so conceited as to think she was interested in him and fought the pathetic little voice that kept saying she must really believe in him if she wanted him to father her baby.

It wasn't as though there were a whole lot of other choices around Forever.

Well, there was Derek, he supposed.

He glanced sharply at Robin. And who was she talking to right now? None other than his good friend Derek.

Maybe she wasn't hanging around the job site in shorts and a dirt smudge to arouse *Jake's* interest. After all, Derek was here, too. And he was a good-looking, successful businessman.

Play The **Lucky Hearts** Game

and get...

FREE BOOKS & a **FREE GIFT...**
YOURS to KEEP!

yes! I have scratched off the silver card.
Please send me my **2 FREE BOOKS**
and **FREE MYSTERY GIFT**. I understand
that I am under no obligation to purchase any
books as explained on the back of this card.

Scratch Here!
*then look below to see
what your cards get you...*

342 HDL DC5V   **142 HDL DC5M**

NAME   (PLEASE PRINT CLEARLY)

ADDRESS

APT.#   CITY

STATE/PROV.   ZIP/POSTAL CODE

Twenty-one gets you
2 FREE BOOKS and a
FREE MYSTERY GIFT!

Twenty gets you
2 FREE BOOKS!

Nineteen gets you
1 FREE BOOK!

TRY AGAIN!

Offer limited to one per household and not valid to current
Harlequin Temptation® subscribers. All orders subject to approval.

Visit us online at
www.eHarlequin.com

(H-T-OS-09/01)   DETACH AND MAIL CARD TODAY!

© 1998 HARLEQUIN ENTERPRISES, LTD. ® and TM are
trademarks owned by Harlequin Enterprises Limited.

The Harlequin Reader Service® — Here's how it works:

Accepting your 2 free books and gift places you under no obligation to buy anything. You may keep the books and gift and return the shipping statement marked "cancel." If you do not cancel, about a month later we'll send you 4 additional novels and bill you just $3.34 each in the U.S., or $3.80 each in Canada, plus 25¢ shipping & handling per book and applicable taxes if any.* That's the complete price and — compared to cover prices of $3.99 each in the U.S. and $4.50 each in Canada — it's quite a bargain! You may cancel at any time, but if you choose to continue, every month we'll send you 4 more books, which you may either purchase at the discount price or return to us and cancel your subscription.

*Terms and prices subject to change without notice. Sales tax applicable in N.Y. Canadian residents will be charged applicable provincial taxes and GST.

Jake didn't know which upset him more: the thought that she might make a play for Derek right under his nose, or that she'd test his resolve by continuing to make a play for *him*.

She laughed at something Derek said and tossed her hair behind her shoulder. She gestured to the top center of the steel frame with both arms. The action pulled her T-shirt over her rib cage, revealing her cute navel and flat stomach.

Jake's hand tightened around the wrench. He closed his eyes and shook his head. He couldn't take much more of this.

Her laughter floated on the breeze.

When he glanced over, she caught his eye. Her sultry smile sent blood rushing to his groin.

He swore. This had to stop before he went crazy. Unable to stand the torment a second longer, he rammed the wrench into his tool belt and stalked over to confront her.

She took a step back at his rapid approach. "Jake?"

Derek, Annie and Connie all turned to look at him curiously. Their faces blurred in his tunnel vision.

He stopped in front of Robin and whispered harshly, "Give up, because it's not going to work."

"What's not going to work?" asked Connie, glancing from Jake's angry face to Robin's puzzled one.

He ignored Connie and stared at Robin.

Her eyes widened in comprehension. "Can we talk *later?*" she asked, face paling a shade.

"No." Jake shook his head firmly. "There won't be a later. Got that?"

Her mouth dropped open.

"Is something wrong, Jake?" asked Derek.

"No. Nothing's wrong." Satisfied his message was delivered, Jake turned to stalk away.

"Jake." Robin's footsteps whispered through the grass as she rushed up behind him.

"Just take your short-shorts, your tight top and your smudged cheek and pick on some other guy." He quickened his pace.

"Jake, they think you're crazy."

"I'm not the crazy one."

"Will you just stand still and have a civil conversation with me?" She grabbed for his arm.

He shook her off. "No."

"They're going to think we're fighting."

"We *are* fighting."

"Jacob Bronson, unless you want me to get grilled by both Connie and Annie you will stop right there and talk to me."

He came to an abrupt halt. She bumped into his back. Her shoulder burned straight through his clothing, and he sucked in a harsh breath. She was right. He turned to face her.

"I'm going to stand here for one minute," he said. "I'm going to say nothing but nonsense. I'm going to smile. You're going to laugh. Everyone watching so avidly over there will think everything is fine. Then we'll go our separate ways." He focused on the river behind her.

"Jake, if you'll just give me a chance to—"

"Talk nonsense, Robin."

"But—"

"Nonsense, or I walk away now and let them grill you." He was bluffing, of course. He no more wanted Robin grilled than she did. He could see now that confronting her in a public place was a mistake. But he sure wasn't about to confront her in private. He might be stupid, but he wasn't suicidal.

"Jake."

He gave in to temptation and looked into her eyes. Their blue-green river depths shimmered at him, begging him to dive in.

"Please?" she asked.

"No."

"Just give me a chance to—"

"You don't understand." His voice hissed as the disheartening truth smacked him square in the chest. It forced the breath right out of him. "If I give you the slightest chance..."

He paused. The wind ruffled her sun-streaked hair, and even now he had to fight the urge to reach for her.

The deck was stacked so completely against him. He sucked up his frustration and tried again. "The slightest chance, and it'll be a done deal."

"Would that be so bad?"

So bad? So *bad*? Didn't she get it?

If she left town carrying his child, she might as well just rip his heart out and cart it around with her for a few years. He'd never be satisfied with another woman. And no future children could possibly take the place of his firstborn.

"Laugh, Robin." Jake forced a painful smile. "Your one minute is up."

7

ROBIN HAD WASTED more than just her minute. She'd also blown a great opportunity to help Jake see reason. She had forty-eight fertile hours left. But, judging by his bullheaded attitude, she wasn't going to make much use of them. She shook a packet of sugar into her steaming teacup at the Fireweed Café.

What was it they said? You could lead a horse to water, but you couldn't make him drink. Well, she'd more than led Jake to water last night. If he still didn't want to drink, there wasn't much more she could do.

She'd have to head back to Toronto on Monday and think about finding another father for her child. The thought depressed her. Now that she'd pictured their children, she didn't want anyone but Jake.

Maybe if she gave him a day to think about it he'd change his mind. Maybe once he'd had a chance to calm down a bit, and really think about all that she could offer a baby, he'd agree to help her have one.

For now, given his volatile mood, the best thing she could do was to stay out of his way for the next twenty-four hours.

"I'll take tea, too," Annie called cheerfully to the waitress as she plunked down across from Robin in the booth. "The helium tank and balloons will be on today's flight," Annie reported.

"That's great." Robin mustered an enthusiastic smile. The party decorations were going to be fantastic. She'd focus on Grandma's party for the rest of the day. And if Jake hadn't changed his mind by tomorrow...well, that was his choice. It wouldn't be the end of the world, just a really big disappointment.

The bell above the glass door tinkled as Derek and Jake walked in.

"Hey, Robin. Hi, Annie." Derek navigated his way around the café tables and slipped into the booth, next to Annie. Jake hesitated beside the table. He peered down at Robin as if she were a coiled snake.

Good grief, she wasn't about to ravish him in the middle of the café.

"The van der Pols absolutely loved you." Derek grinned at Robin as he signaled to the waitress.

"Coffee, Derek? Jake?" The waitress set Annie's tea down, looking expectantly at the two men.

"Sure," Jake replied somewhat fatalistically, folding his big body to perch on the very edge of the bench. He flipped over the stoneware mug.

"Bring me a burger," said Derek, turning his own cup so the waitress could fill it. "You had lunch yet, ladies?"

Robin nodded. "Tea's fine for me."

"I'm good, too," said Annie.

Robin glanced from Annie to Derek and back again. If their dance last night had spurred a romance, they weren't showing it. They seemed perfectly relaxed sitting next to one another—rather like old friends.

"Anything for you, Jake?" asked the waitress.

"No thanks." His deep voice was tight with tension.

"You sick, buddy?" asked Derek.

"Just not hungry." Jake's fingers drummed on the tabletop, and Robin could feel the vibration from his foot tapping on the floor.

His hostility was getting ridiculous. He was practically hanging off his end of the bench. It wasn't as if she'd get pregnant from sitting within a foot of him. As Derek and Annie handed their menus to the waitress, Robin leaned toward Jake.

"Don't sulk," she whispered out of the corner of her mouth.

"I'm not sulking," he hissed.

"What was that?" Derek glanced from one to the other.

"I was asking Jake why he's not having lunch."

"Quit obsessing about my lunch."

"What lunch?" asked Derek on a laugh.

Annie smiled at Derek's joke.

Jake glared at Derek.

"Back to the van der Pols," said Derek to Robin. "I'm taking them out to see the russet trees today, and I was hoping you'd come with us."

"Down the river?" She sipped her tea, deciding to

ignore Jake's hostility. Hopefully it would burn itself out.

"Down to Hillstock Valley," Derek explained. "We'll do the creek trail, then have a picnic on the beach. They're keen to experience the great outdoors and get some pictures of the harvesting methods. Environmentally friendly practices really help sell products in Europe right now. So, what do you say, Robin? Care to come along and translate?"

Robin looked over at Annie, who was methodically stirring her tea. "Why don't you take Annie along?"

Derek glanced sideways at his accounting clerk. "Annie can't translate."

"I know, but I've got a couple of things I need to do still this afternoon. Why don't you take Annie along and I'll catch up with you all later?"

Jake snorted softly beside her.

Robin resisted an urge to elbow him in the ribs. Just because he was going to be stuck with Snake Woman, didn't mean Derek didn't deserve a chance with Annie.

"Want to come along, Annie?" asked Derek.

"Sure." Annie smiled, but Robin still couldn't tell if her matchmaking efforts were paying off. They could have been brother and sister for all the reaction she got.

"What time will you be finished?" asked Derek.

Robin shrugged. "Maybe three?"

"You could meet us there for an afternoon picnic," he suggested hopefully.

"Sure." The van der Pols were very nice people, and Robin hadn't been up to see the russet trees in years. Besides, she wanted to give Jake a little room to breathe. She glanced sideways at his tense expression. Okay, a lot of room to breathe.

Maybe he'd remember that of all the men in the world, she'd asked him to father her child. It was a compliment not an insult.

"We're taking the runabout, but you can come up in the freighter canoe," said Derek.

"It has a motor, right?" she confirmed.

"Of course it does. I wouldn't make you paddle. Shouldn't take you more that forty-five minutes."

"In that case, I'd be happy to meet you."

IT WAS THREE-THIRTY before Robin set off down the Forever River in Derek's freighter canoe. Twenty-one feet from stem to stern, the boat was heavy and rode low in the water.

She rounded the first bend and putted past the girl's beach. Water lapped quietly on the shore. The poplar leaves had turned golden with the early northern frosts, and the cranberry bushes were brilliant red against the perennial green of the spruce trees. She'd forgotten how beautiful the bush became in the early fall.

She could almost hear the echo of children's laughter and wondered if graduating classes still went skinny-dipping after the dance. She hoped they did.

She passed a small tributary. Fox Creek, if she remembered correctly. Then she pointed her canoe down the center of the wide river. Aided by the current, the miles flew by. When she came to the place where the river forked, she took the left fork, down the Hillstock Valley.

She came across a beaver lodge and saw two of the flat-tailed, furry animals dragging freshly cut poplar trees through the water. Robin let out a deep sigh. Over the years, she'd forgotten the exceptional peace of Forever.

A few miles later, as an eagle cried overhead, a vague feeling of disquiet assailed her.

Nothing had changed. Well, the river was getting narrower, and the water was getting louder and rougher as it flowed around boulders that poked up through the surface. But there was something else, something she couldn't quite put her finger on.

She glanced around at the bush, then into the treetop, then across the distant mountains. That was it. On the north horizon, where Sheep Mountain should have been, there was nothing but sky and developing thunderheads.

Her stomach clenched. She wasn't *in* the Hillstock Valley. She must have taken the wrong channel. But how was that possible?

Frowning, she veered toward the shore to give herself enough space to turn the canoe and backtrack. This was going to be embarrassing. She wished she knew where she'd made the mistake.

She shifted the tiller on the small outboard motor

and cranked the throttle to make a tight turn. Halfway around, the boat lurched awkwardly. The motor whined, then clunked, then was quiet as the boat sucked to a stop on a hidden sandbar.

Robin gaped over the edge of the canoe, mumbling a mild curse when she saw the sand and pea gravel six inches under the surface. Now what was she going to do?

The water was deep and swift on either side of the sandbar, roaring relentlessly in her ears. She would get swept away in the current and die of hypothermia if she tried to get to shore. The motor was buried in sand, and it really hadn't sounded too healthy when it shut down.

She considered stepping into the shallow water of the sandbar to try to free the motor. But what if it didn't start again? She'd be dragged further down the river with nothing but a short emergency paddle to steer with. There were numerous rocks to avoid, and...

She tipped her head to one side and tried to listen carefully. Was the water getting louder?

She shaded her eyes, scanning the river. Her jaw dropped. Her hand fell to her lap, and she sent up a quick, silent prayer for the motor to remain firmly anchored to the sandbar.

Fifty feet downstream, the river dropped away. There was a waterfall ahead. It was a rather large waterfall, judging by the hollow roar and the backspray sparkling up into the sunshine.

Robin sat very still, concentrating on remaining calm and taking stock of the situation. She was trained in all kinds of emergency procedures. This wasn't the first time an adventure had taken an unexpected turn. Though it was the first time she'd been completely alone when it happened.

She was only alone temporarily, she reminded herself. Other people knew where she was. Well, they sort of knew where she was. They knew she was on the river, anyway. Plus, she was overdue.

She glanced at her watch. Derek had expected her at least forty-five minutes ago. When she didn't show up, he'd come looking for her.

And there was more good news. The canoe felt very stable on the sandbar. She couldn't get to shore, but that was fine. The only advantage in getting to shore was to build a fire. Realistically, all she had to do was sit and wait, wait and stay warm.

The spray from the waterfall quickly soaked through the sleeves of her sweater. Not good, but not a disaster, either. Her lifejacket was waterproof and would at least keep her torso warm.

She rubbed her damp face with the palm of her hand. The waterfall spray was her biggest problem. Nothing sapped body heat faster than wet hair and wet clothing. Again, she took stock of the situation. If she crouched down in the bottom of the canoe, the sides would help protect her from both the wind and the mist.

So, taking care not to jiggle the motor, she shifted

her rear end off the canoe seat. She braced her hands on the crossbar and lowered herself to the floor. The canoe shifted to one side, and a trapped puddle of icy water whooshed across the bottom, soaking her shorts.

She gasped and sprang back up.

The canoe tilted.

She grabbed the gunwales. After a breathless second, the boat stabilized. Then she gingerly put her weight back down on the seat, determined to not move again.

Recovering from the shock, she breathed a sigh of relief. The canoe hadn't broken free.

The wind shifted, and the waterfall spray blew sideways and away from her. Things were looking up. There was still some heat left in the setting sun, and Derek would arrive in no time.

Robin settled herself for a wait.

A branch on shore snapped, echoing across the river. She turned swiftly toward the noise. Another cracking sound came from the brush. The red cranberry bushes on the edge of the rocky beach shook.

Her mouth dropped open as a grizzly bear ambled out of the forest cover. So much for things looking up.

The bear was round and burly. His thick glossy coat rippled with the shift of muscle as he wandered toward the water. He waded in, not fifty feet away. Robin instinctively pulled back toward the opposite end of the canoe. The bear stopped, belly-deep in the rushing current. He stuck his nose through the surface, eyes fixed on the water.

Suddenly he lunged forward, jaws snapping. Robin's heartbeat thundered in her chest. The bear raised its dripping head with a big red salmon trapped between his sharp teeth. Then he pivoted on his hind legs and galloped to shore.

While he ripped into the fish, Robin gasped a few rapid breaths. She cautiously lowered herself to the bottom of the boat. Given a choice between the freezing water and being spotted by a grizzly, she'd take the water any day of the week.

Her teeth chattered, and the clunky lifejacket made it difficult to get comfortable, but she still figured hiding was her best option.

She'd obviously cruised up a salmon spawning tributary. The national park service had done numerous bear studies in Forever when she was a child. She didn't remember any fatalities.

Grizzlies busy salmon fishing were unlikely to bother humans. At least, that's what the wildlife biologists claimed. But she figured a grizzly was even less likely to bother a human that he couldn't see.

She started to tremble more vigorously against the cold canoe bottom and realized hypothermia was setting in. She pushed her shirt cuff out of the way and tried to focus on her watch. The numbers were blurry, but she thought two hours had passed since she got stuck.

Where, oh, where, was Derek?

She curled up as best she could around the life-jacket. Her legs were freezing, her feet going numb. The wind had picked up and she could hear thunder in the distance. The waterfall spray rained down on her, soaking her hair.

Of all the places she'd traveled, all the adventures that had taken her to dangerous and exciting spots around the world, wouldn't it be ironic to have it all end in the Forever River, twenty miles from where she was born?

She chuckled weakly. Her fingers were starting to tingle. Either she was colder than she felt, or her cramped position was cutting off the circulation. She pondered the question for a moment, but then gave up trying to figure out which it was.

Her brain was sluggish, and it wasn't as if she could do anything about either case. The thunder rumbled again, closer this time.

JAKE GAZED at the storm clouds on the horizon, glad to have the tent finished well in advance of the rain.

"The tent looks great." Connie stepped up on the picnic table bench and took a seat beside him on the tabletop. Their perch overlooked the narrow strip of rocky beach and the town dock.

"Should be a good party," said Jake. He scanned down the river waiting for a glimpse of Derek's boat. In his estimation, they should have been back by now.

"My kids can't wait." Connie flipped her wind-blown hair out of her face.

Jake grinned. He couldn't wait for the party, either. When he was a child, he'd loved the big town barbe-cues and square dances. They were timeless magical evenings where everyone belonged and everyone had fun. It was part of what he wanted for his own children.

The bow of a boat rounded the curve in the river. Jake's stomach muscles relaxed. Finally, they were back.

"Is that Annie with Derek?" asked Connie, squint-ing at the passengers in the little runabout.

"Yeah." Jake stood. "Annie and a couple of the European buyers."

"Did you notice the two of them dancing at your party?"

"Annie and Derek?"

"Yeah."

"Sure." Jake shrugged.

Connie's laughter tinkled in the open air. "Look at Mrs. Pennybrooke down on the river path. She's spotted Derek and Annie. Oh, wait. She's stopping, gaping, appraising."

Jake shook his head. He could almost hear Mrs. Pennybrooke's synapses revving from here. "That's our small town," he muttered.

"Some things never change," said Connie. "What do you bet that the Forever Pioneer Ladies have started a wedding quilt by tonight."

"A guy can't even dance in this town," said Jake.

"A guy can't put out a personal ad for a wife and *then* dance," said Connie.

"The personal ad was for me." Jake watched Derek tie up the boat. His gaze then returned to the bend in the river, waiting for Robin to appear. His stomach muscles started to tighten up again.

"Everybody knows Derek put it there." Connie jumped down from the table. "Better go get the kids."

"Yeah. Sure. See you later." Jake took a step toward the dock. Where the heck was Robin?

"'Bye, Jake." Connie headed for the playground.

Derek helped the van der Pols out of the boat, then reached down and extended a hand for Annie. Jake vaguely noted that Annie had been jumping agilely in and out of motorboats for the past three decades, but he didn't have time to give that observation much thought. He returned his attention to the river bend.

Any minute now...

Robin would appear with the canoe...

He waited. And waited...

He let out a frustrated breath and strode across the park to the gravel of River Front Road.

He greeted the van der Pols with a nod and a tight smile as they left the dock, then continued on to where Derek was unpacking the boat.

"Where's Robin?" Jake came to a stop beside a small pile of lifejackets and coolers. He stripped off his gloves, tucking them into the back pockets of his jeans. He reached for the red fuel tank Derek was lift-ing out of the bottom of the boat.

"Never showed." Derek handed Jake the half-full tank. "Figured you guys were still working on the decorations."

"What do you mean, she never showed?" A sick feeling clenched in the pit of his stomach as he set the heavy metal tank down on the dock.

"We waited. She didn't come." Derek stopped working to peer quizzically up at Jake.

"Jake?" Annie fixed him with a worried stare.

Jake was not going to panic. There was definitely going to be a logical explanation for this. What were the odds that Robin was in trouble?

"You mean, she isn't here?" asked Annie.

"She left about three-thirty." Jake glared down the river. If this was a ploy to play on his white-knight tendencies, he would...

Derek left the rest of his gear and vaulted quickly out of the boat. He clasped Annie's hand.

"Oh, no." Annie's voice was strained, and she moved closer to Derek.

Jake cursed under his breath. Robin wouldn't do something like this just to get his attention. Would she?

What did he know? He hadn't seen the woman in fifteen years. All he knew about her was that she was a brilliant knockout with a good sense of humor. And she really wanted to have a baby.

Just how badly did she want a baby? How far would she go to achieve her goal?

Derek took a step toward shore. "I'll get Patrick and the boys."

"Don't." Jake stopped Derek with a hand on his arm. If there was a chance he was being set up, he sure didn't want to cause a panic. And the last thing in the world he needed was for this small town to know what was going on between him and Robin.

"Why not?" Derek was clearly confused.

"We have to find her," said Annie.

"Let me go look alone."

"Are you nuts?" asked Derek.

Annie's eyes widened.

"Just give me a couple of hours. We know where she was headed. It's not very cold. If she's not in the river..."

He didn't even want to *think* about the possibility of Robin falling in the river. She was toying with him. She had to be.

He cleared his throat. "She's probably on a beach somewhere, out of gas, and perfectly fine."

"And if she's in the river?" Derek stared at him intently.

Jake slid an apologetic look toward Annie before focusing on Derek. "Then more boats aren't going to help."

Derek swore. He wrapped a comforting arm around Annie.

"I don't want to panic her family," said Jake. "Especially not her grandmother. Annie—" he reached out to rub Annie's shoulder "—I'm sure Robin is fine. I'm going to find her. Okay?"

Annie nodded.

"Two hours," Derek agreed.

AN HOUR LATER Jake was vacillating between terror and rage. If this was a trick, he was going to kill her. If she'd gone into the river, he didn't know what he'd do.

He closed his eyes briefly against the intense horror the thought evoked. Robin was fine. She had to be fine. Anything else was unthinkable.

He should never have let her make the trip on her own. It had been fifteen years since she'd navigated the river. He'd been stupid and irresponsible to stay in town just because he was afraid he couldn't resist her.

Of course he could resist her. She was just a woman, for goodness' sake. Just a flesh-and-blood woman. She wasn't even his fantasy anymore. She'd blown that when she tried to steal his baby.

He'd covered every inch of the river between town and the Hillstock Valley. He'd checked the beaches, the coves and every navigable tributary.

No Robin.

He zoomed past the valley in the hope that she'd somehow missed it and turned up the next branch of the river. He couldn't imagine how she'd missed the channel, but he was running out of options.

Jake gunned the engine and sent Derek's runabout skimming along the surface of the narrow arm, hoping against hope to find her lounging on a blanket with a beach fire burning and a come-hither look in her eyes. He'd come hither, all right, but she was going to wish he hadn't.

He turned the outboard to round a steep corner, cutting back on power because of the rocks sticking out of the water. It was a long shot that she'd come this way. He knew it was a long shot, but he simply wasn't ready to conclude they needed to start an all-out search. He didn't think he could bring himself to dredge the river.

He sucked in a breath of cold air. She was all right, he told himself for the thousandth time. She'd survived Thailand, she *would* survive the Forever River.

When he passed a grizzly bear fishing near the shore, his worry ratcheted up another notch. He hadn't thought about bears. He'd been too busy worrying about drowning and exposure.

His hand tightened on the throttle. He zigged and zagged around rocks and shallow spots. The clouds were closing overhead, flattening the light, making it hard to navigate.

When he spotted Derek's faded red canoe, Jake's emotions rocketed from relief to fury to panic. It was stationary, lodged on a sandbar in the middle of the river just above the falls. But Robin wasn't in it.

His body turned ice-cold.

She wasn't in the boat.

He gunned the engine, frantically searching the shoreline for signs of her. He cringed as he scanned the scene for her body, then swallowed past the cold terror in his throat as he looked more closely for drag marks.

His vision blurred. For a second he thought his mind might just shut down.

8

AS HE GOT CLOSER something moved in the bottom of the canoe. A flash of life jacket, a hand on the gunwale, and her wet hair as she rose unsteadily to a sitting position.

Thank you, thank you, thank you.

She looked to be hurt, but she was alive.

Jake slowed the bigger boat, idling up alongside the sandbar that had her trapped.

"You okay?" he called, residual terror rasping his voice.

She nodded, pausing to rest on the seat. Her hair was dripping, her clothing soaked, and her eyes looked glazed.

"I can't reach you," he called, cranking tiller and reversing the engine to keep the craft level with her. "It's too shallow over there. I'll throw you a rope."

She nodded uncertainly, blinking slowly at him. He wasn't sure she heard him.

"Are you all right?" he repeated. She looked half drowned and half frozen. If her slow movements and apparent brain functions were anything to go by, she was severely hypothermic. Either that or traumatized.

He couldn't reach her with the boat, and didn't dare go into the water to get her. If he got swept away by the current—a virtual certainty in this part of the river—they'd have two casualties on their hands. He berated himself for not bringing Derek.

Why did he have to be so suspicious of her? What had she done that was so terrible? Sure, she'd tried to get pregnant, but that wasn't exactly a crime. He should have known she wouldn't stage a disappearance.

"Can you catch a rope?" he asked again, not about to let her die of his hardheaded stupidity.

She nodded this time, and held out an unsteady hand. Good. He made a loop knot at the end of the rope, both to give it weight and to make it easier for her to tie off. Then he tossed the knotted end gently, placing it right in the center of the canoe.

She crawled over and picked it up.

"Way to go!" He celebrated the small victory. The sooner he got her out of there, the better. The spray was making her wetter by the second. "Now tie it to the bow."

She glanced at the end of the rope, and looked up at the bow of the boat. He could almost feel her bracing herself for the journey. He desperately wanted to help her. He held his breath, clenching his muscles as she slowly covered every excruciating inch of the canoe.

When she finally made it to the bow, she shakily tried to thread the rope through the eyelet. The rope slipped from her clumsy fingers. She couldn't do it. Her hands were shaking too badly.

She rubbed them together, bit her lip, and tried again.

She dropped the rope again. It was almost too painful to watch as she picked it up for another try.

"Take your time," he called in an effort to calm her. Though inwardly he prayed she'd hurry.

He didn't like the way her weight was tipping the canoe, working the leg of the motor up and down in the loose sand. She'd lose her moorage soon. If that happened, there would be nothing between her and the waterfall.

He glanced toward the falls.

No way, no how. It was simply not going to happen. He was here, and he would get her out. If he had to jump in the water, he'd jump in the damn water. Robin was *not* going to die today.

She threaded the rope.

His knees nearly buckled with relief. All she had to do was to knot it. Any knot. Surely to goodness an adventure woman knew a hundred knots.

She twisted the end of the rope around itself, frowned, then pulled it apart and tried again.

"Through my loop," he called, steadying his boat against the uneven current.

"Through the loop!" His hands automatically made the motions for a knot. She could do it. He knew she could do it.

"I can't..." She gave her head a little shake, as if to clear her vision. He had to get her warm.

She squinted at her hands, pushed the end of the rope through one more loop and leaned back from the bow. "Okay," she sighed uncertainly.

They didn't have any time to waste. The canoe shifted on the sandbar and pivoted toward the falls. Jake turned his boat and gently revved the engine, making sure he didn't stress her knot. Slowly, painstakingly, the canoe turned toward his stern.

He willed the knot to hold as he dragged her toward the shore. He beached his boat and rushed to the back to pull her in. The nylon rope was frigid against his palms as he kept a steady pressure against her knot.

He could only imagine how cold she was from sitting in the spray for hours.

He stretched his hand out and grabbed the cold metal gunwale with his fingertips. He reeled it in and retied her precarious knot. Then he grasped her in his arms and lifted her into the boat.

She was a stumbling mass of shivers as he hauled her over the stern. His arms took on a will of their own, and once he got hold of her he couldn't let her go.

Her lips were blue, her eyes glazed, and she was soaked to the skin. It was going to take them half an hour to get back to town, half an hour of her dripping wet in the windy open boat.

After a long minute of simply holding her close, he

regained enough sense to strip off her life jacket. She stood still as he efficiently removed her wet top. Then he covered her in his flannel shirt.

It was dry and still warm from his body heat. But it wasn't going to be enough. He had to get her near a serious heat source, and fast.

He had to get a fire going on the beach. He'd rather have her inside a house, better still, in a warm bath, but he didn't want to risk the boat trip back while she was in this condition.

He helped her onto the beach, then started a fire with the sun-dried wood strewn around the shore.

The fire caught quickly and crackled satisfyingly as it grew in leaps and bounds.

Jake used his T-shirt to dry her hair. Then he cradled her between his legs, facing the warm fire. His body protected her from the wind and reflected the fire's heat toward her.

"You okay?" He brushed her damp hair back from her chilled face, gently toweling her cheeks and neck.

She nodded, teeth chattering, an unexpected excitement in her voice. "Did you see the bear?"

"Yeah." He wrapped both arms around her.

She shook her head. "I'd forgotten how exciting it can be on the Forever River."

"Exciting?"

"Well. Scary, I guess. I hid from the bear."

"Good idea."

"Yeah." Her teeth started to chatter in earnest. "I'm *so* cold."

"I know. We'll sit tight here until you get warm. Derek might start looking for us, but that's okay. I'd rather have them worry than have you drop unconscious on me halfway home."

"Am I that far gone?" She rested her head against his bare chest, it jiggled as she shook with cold.

"You're going to be fine."

She sighed between convulsive shivers. "I'm so glad you're here."

"I'm glad I'm here, too," he whispered. Grateful that'd he found her. Grateful that she was safe.

He couldn't think of anyplace else in the world he'd rather be than sitting on a windswept beach with Robin safe and sound in his arms.

"Tell me about your new job." Though the fire and his own body heat were starting to warm her, Jake knew it was a good idea to keep her talking and alert.

"I'll be the manager of Mixed Tour Coordination section."

"'Mixed Tour'?" He reached around her to toss another thick stick on the glowing fire.

"Wild Ones is developing a series of quasi-adventure tours."

"What's a quasi-adventure?"

"Adventures for people who aren't in top physical condition. We want to combine the excitement of an outdoor adventure, with a higher level of creature comfort and five-star cuisine." She sounded as if she were quoting a brochure.

"Action for rich, out-of-shape people?"

Robin elbowed him in the ribs. "Not exactly. Not everyone is capable of climbing Everest."

"I know I'm not."

"See, there. You might just be our demographic. Instead of having a tour group carry their packs up a mountainside, we'll have them hike the mountain, but have a lodge and a chef, and maybe a hot tub, waiting for them at the top."

"Sounds good to me so far."

"All the fun, without all the deprivation. Of course we'll still offer the climb-mountains, sleep-on-rocks, eat-gruel tours for the purists."

"I think the quasi ones sound better." He chuckled, relieved that her shaking was starting to abate.

"There's definitely a market for both."

"Do you test the quasi-adventure tours?"

She shook her head. "I'll be in the Toronto office. The location scouts will submit their reports to me, and I'll package the new tours and design the marketing campaigns."

"Sounds like fun."

"I'm looking forward to it."

"Good." He nodded. "That's good." He couldn't keep the bleak hollow sound from his voice. Robin was going back to Toronto to start an exciting new life. There was nothing for her in Forever. Nothing he could offer to compete with her career.

"Tell me about you," she suggested. "Why did you pick bucking horses?"

"I always wanted to be a cowboy as a kid. I guess I just never grew up."

"You grew up just fine, Jake." Her voice was husky. She stared directly into the bright orange fire.

He cleared his throat. "Yeah. Well, the other reason is that my grandfather wanted his ranch to be a legacy. Dad never did anything with it, so I decided it was up to me."

"You're honoring your grandfather?"

"Only partly. The soil is better suited to livestock feed than market vegetables. Besides, I love breeding horses." The last sliver of sun dipped behind the jagged mountain range to the west, and the flames suddenly grew brighter.

"How many horses do you have?"

"Probably about forty of them are here right now." Jake did a quick mental calculation. Forty was about right.

"Where are the rest?"

"I also have some land in northern Alberta—"

"Really?" She suddenly turned to stare at him.

He braced himself for her to ask why he didn't move to Alberta. No matter what she said, he wasn't going to start another argument. He waited, but she just silently blinked those big, beautiful eyes.

"Most of the horses winter in Alberta," he continued, to keep himself from leaning in and kissing her. "I have a great manager, and a group of wranglers that take them to various rodeos around North America."

"Do you ever go out to the rodeos?"

"Occasionally. Mostly I stay here and focus on the breeding program."

"And ride the wild bucking broncos," she joked, settling back against his chest. The wind was starting to chill his bare back, but he steeled himself against the cold. He could sit here all night long and protect her if need be.

"Sometimes," he agreed with a smile. "But it's a young man's sport."

"You're not old."

"I'm not young, either." Which is why he wanted to get married and start a family.

He checked that thought. It was going to take a while to reconcile himself to a wife other than Robin. And no way in the world could he contemplate it while he held her in his arms. It was time to change the subject.

"Tell me what happened out there with the canoe." He resolved to concentrate on the here and now. He tightened his hold on her. Here and now was about as good as it got in his opinion.

"I took a wrong turn." Her body was warming, and she felt so *right* cuddled up against his chest.

Jake rested his chin on the top of her head. Here and now was all he'd ever wanted. A warm fire, Robin and Forever. Why was it so impossible?

He refused to allow himself to get maudlin. "I gathered you took a wrong turn. How did you get stuck?"

"I took another wrong turn."

"Cute."

She sighed. "I thought I'd remember the river, but it looks really different when you've been away." She tipped her head up to look at him again, blue-green eyes exotically beautiful in the waning light. "Thanks for coming after me."

"Anytime," he whispered hoarsely. He focused on her lips. The color had returned to them and they were lush and tempting in the shifting orange shadows. Unable to resist, he tipped his head toward her.

Her lips parted with a little puff of air. He moved in, closer still, slowly gauging her reaction, watching for any sign of resistance. There was none.

Her breath fanned sweetly against his face as he crossed the final inch that separated them.

The kiss was long and sweet and desperate and relieved. There was none of the hard-edged lust that had hijacked his senses last night. Her tender kiss and the feel of her cuddled in his arms fueled a slow aching burn today.

"You're such a gentleman, Jake," she whispered.

He smiled. But it was a melancholy smile. He didn't want to be her gentleman. He wanted to be her reckless adventure, her lover, her life.

"Anytime, Robin." He smoothed her drying hair back from her face. Then he gave her a gentleman's kiss, sweet and chaste compared to their others. It was also a kiss of regret and a kiss of goodbye. Because Jake knew instinctively that this was the last time he'd hold her in his arms.

He could already hear an outboard motor in the distance, and he gathered Robin to him. The world was closing in, and he was going to lose her for good.

ROBIN CURLED UP in her mother's big armchair. Dressed in loose-fitting sweatpants and a comfortable pullover sweater, she was finally warm again. A fire crackled in the big stone fireplace, and she slowly sipped a mug of hot chocolate. She had to admit, it felt kind of good to have her family clucking over her. She'd been living on her own for a long time now.

Since Derek had sent up an alarm when Jake hadn't returned in the allotted two hours, her family had been wreathed in smiles when she'd shown up safe and sound. Jake had left immediately, seeming embarrassed by their effusive gratitude. Now she wondered what he was doing next door in his big house. She wished he'd stayed.

"Mrs. Winklemyer and the Giant Fish," called Bobbie, dashing into the living room and jumping onto the long couch, a book clutched in his hand. Freshly bathed, his hair curled across his forehead in a damp cowlick.

"Slow down, buckaroo," called Robert. Robin's burly brother-in-law ambled into the living room with his other two sons in tow.

"Wait for me," Connie called from the kitchen.

Robin leaned back, enjoying the antics of her nephews as they jockeyed for position around their father.

"Here, Mommy. Here, Mommy." Bobbie patted the cushion next to him.

Connie sat, sandwiching Bobbie between his parents. Bobbie sighed and leaned his head on his father's beefy shoulder so he could see the book. One little hand reached up to twirl a lock of hair on his forehead, the other stroked Connie's forearm. An expression of pure bliss wreathed his face.

Robin's heart contracted. The joy she felt for her nephew was tempered with sadness for herself. Her arms felt empty. She wanted a small, warm child curled trustingly and lovingly against her. And she wanted to go back to this afternoon when Jake's embrace made her feel as though she had a special place in the world.

She had a sudden wild urge to dash over to his house and toss herself into his arms.

But she couldn't do that. They'd taken the first steps toward a truce and a real friendship this afternoon. And she still held out hope that he'd change his mind about helping her have a baby. She needed to give him some time alone. There was too much at risk.

A little dark-haired boy would fit so nicely in her lap. As Robert's deep voice started the story, she closed her eyes and imagined.

THE FESTIVAL TENT GLOWED with the lights of a hundred oil lamps. Replete from the potluck dinner, Jake sipped a glass of punch as he gazed around the elaborately decorated space.

In the center of the tent, Derek's carpenters had built a large dance floor, which was surrounded by dozens of tables. To cover the tables, ladies had donated tablecloths of every size and color.

Patrick Moore and the swing band were tuning up on a low stage in one corner. Dweedle-Dumb paced back and forth in front of them, and guests all gave the dog a wide berth. Jake chuckled. Patrick could probably rent Dweedle out as security for any number of rock stars.

The dinner had been cleared away, "Happy Birthday" had been sung at the top of everyone's lungs three times over, and Alma May was cutting her giant wild-rose cake. A quick lineup formed in front of the head table as the town children vied for a piece of cake with a plump icing rosebud on top.

Sitting on the sideline with Derek, Jake watched Robin and Connie dole out napkins and paper plates. Eunice presided over the cake with a laughing Alma May. Robin's grandmother was clearly enjoying her party.

Jake's gaze slid back to Robin. Drop-dead gorgeous in a sleeveless, formfitting, silver dress, her hair was loosely pinned up on her head, soft curls caressing her cheeks. The neckline was high, but there was an interesting diamond-shaped cutout over her back that showed off an expanse of creamy skin. She wore tiny sapphire earrings that reflected the light from the oil lamp onto the table in front of her.

Everything about her shimmered and glittered as she bent to trade jokes with the town children. In that outfit, she should have been the perfect Ice Princess. But a sensitivity glowed deep within her, and she looked anything but cold.

As the adults moved up in the cake line, Robin was lost to his view.

A few minutes later notes from the first waltz filled the tent. Parents called their exuberant, balloon-toting children from the dance floor as couples congregated. Derek rose from the chair next to Jake.

"Time for me to find Annie." He grinned.

"I thought dancing with Annie was illegal?" Jake quirked his eyebrows.

"I'm not going to ask her to dance," Derek assured him. "I'm going to stand beside her and tap my foot until she asks me. Nothin' illegal about saying yes." With an impish grin, Derek strode across the tent.

Minutes later he was holding Annie close on the dance floor. Judging by the radiant smile on Annie's face, Derek was one heck of a foot tapper.

He whispered something in her ear, and her smile turned secretive and self-conscious. She pressed her cheek against Derek's chest, and Derek pulled her close. Jake felt a twinge of jealousy as he realized Robin was right, Derek was going to find a wife right here in town.

Annie tipped her head to look adoringly up at Derek. Derek touched her cheek, then leaned forward to kiss her. Jake quickly looked away, feeling like a voyeur. But the other good citizens around Derek and Annie showed no such compunction. They burst into spontaneous applause.

Annie blushed, and Derek grinned. He gave her a quick hug and kissed her forehead. Connie was sure right about the wedding quilt. If the Pioneer Ladies hadn't started it by now, it was on the top of their To Do list for tomorrow morning.

Derek caught Jake's eye, and Jake lifted his glass in a silent toast. The town would have them married within a month.

Jake paused. His eyes narrowed thoughtfully. He set his punch glass down on the table with a clunk.

He was a fool.

He'd been going about this all wrong. Staying away from Robin wasn't the way to make her his. Here in Forever, he needed to stay as close to her as possible.

He needed to dance with her, hold her and kiss her in a very public way. If Robin could use his wet, white dress shirt as a weapon to get his baby, he could use her friends and neighbors as a weapon to get her to marry him and stay in town.

He was sure both techniques were about even on the ethics scale.

He grinned, and rose to his feet. Look out, Ms. Medford. Jake Bronson is about to bring the full power of his and the town's love to bear on your unsuspecting little heart.

He strode across the grass floor with a spring in his step. There he joined the last of the cake lineup.

"End piece, Jake?" asked Eunice.

"No thanks," said Jake. "I'm here to ask your daughter to dance."

Eunice stepped back for a moment. Then she smiled. "Which one?"

Jake grinned. "The one who doesn't have a husband who used to be a linebacker."

"Good choice," said Eunice.

Jake winked and proceeded down the table. "Robin?"

"Yes?" She eyed him hesitantly.

"Dance?" He held out his hand.

She glanced around at her relatives. They all nodded encouragingly, helpful grins on their faces. Jake knew he could count on these people.

But he kept his smile of satisfaction under control. Robin took his hand right there in front of her entire family and various townsfolk gossips. Step One accomplished, and how.

He guided her around the end of the table, then linked their fingers together as they headed for the dance floor.

"Did you see Annie and Derek?" he asked, pulling Robin into his arms. He rested his fingers against the open back of her dress. A warm feeling of satisfaction shuddered through him. She fit his arms so perfectly.

"Where?" She glanced around.

"They're dancing together." He felt her smile. "When I spin you, take a look."

He whirled her around and she peeked over his shoulder. "Wow," she whispered.

He chuckled. "I think it worked."

"It sure did," said Robin. "This is great."

"Yeah. I'm really happy for them." But not as happy as he was going to be for himself. "Is Alma May enjoying herself?"

Robin sighed. "Oh, yeah. It's a great party."

"Glad you came home?"

"Mmm-hmm."

"So am I."

She stiffened for a second. Jake silently congratulated himself on putting her off balance. He wondered what her reaction would be if he blurted out the fact that he loved her. Better to wait on that one, he decided.

He was starting to intercept interested gazes from couples dancing by. They obviously wondered what his intentions were.

Strictly honorable. Well, eventually they'd be strictly honorable. There'd be a bit of subterfuge between now and the honorable part.

He let his fingers trail along the edge of her dress back, enjoying the contrast of her warm skin and the gauzy fabric. Goose bumps rose in reaction to the intimate caress.

He guided her head against his chest. Giving in, she sighed and closed her eyes.

"You look beautiful," he whispered.

"Thank you."

"I mean, stunningly, incredibly, drop-dead gorgeous."

"Always the gentleman," she responded lightly. But he could tell by the way her body softened against him that the sincere compliment had affected her.

He gently kissed the top of her head. Her back was to the dance floor, so she didn't see Mrs. Pennybrooke's penciled eyebrows nearly hit the ceiling. They'd be planning a double wedding any minute now.

"Jake?"

"Yes?" She was going to be his. His, his, his.

"What are you doing after the dance?"

Binding you to me so damn tight you'll never get away. "I don't know. Why?"

"Want to go for a walk or something?"

"Sure."

The song ended, and she pulled back.

"Thanks," she said.

"Thank you." He leaned over and kissed her lightly on the lips.

Her eyes widened, and she quickly glanced around. "Uh, Jake."

"Yeah?'

"They're going to think—"

"Let 'em think whatever they want."

"But—"

"We're adults, Robin. It's none of their business." He pulled her close and started to dance as the band segued into the next song.

Fortunately for him, nobody had ever successfully convinced the Pioneer Ladies that anybody's love life was none of their business. They'd continue operating as if Jake and Robin's love life was entirely their business.

Bless them.

ALMA MAY MADE HER EXIT at eleven. Three dances later, Jake decided the townspeople had had enough of an eyeful of him and Robin. And his body had taken just about as much torment as it could stand. The feel, the scent and the sight of Robin had desire clawing at every nerve ending.

It was time for them to be alone—very, very alone.

They slipped out the back exit into the cool star-studded night. Robin immediately kicked off her high-heeled shoes. Jake reached down and picked them up off the cool grass. Her stocking-covered feet nestled within the long blades sent a bolt of desire right through him.

"Cold?" he asked.

"Not bad." She rubbed her arms.

He shed his suit jacket and draped it across her shoulders.

"Thanks." She smiled.

The sound and lights of the party faded behind them as they strolled along the river in the general direction of his house.

When they were well away from anyone else, Jake turned and drew Robin into his arms. He kissed her soundly. Her response was hot and instantaneous, buckling his knees. He stepped back before he was anywhere near ready and brushed a curl from her forehead.

"So, Robin. You still want to get pregnant?"

9

ROBIN BLINKED. Her jaw dropped open. So much for figuring out how to broach the subject delicately. "Huh?"

"Do you still want to have my baby?" Jake's dark blue eyes burned a secret passion. It certainly looked as though he'd had an opportunity to reconsider.

"Y-yes," she stuttered.

He smiled. "Okay."

"It's okay?" Wait a minute. What the heck was going on here? This was a one-hundred-and-eighty-degree turn with no signal.

"Yeah. It's okay." He took her hands in his, stroking his thumbs along the ridges of her knuckles. "I can honestly say there is nothing I'd rather do right now than make a baby with you."

"But—" She swallowed the rest of the question. Only a fool would start analyzing his motivation. He'd agreed. He'd agreed to help her have a baby. By next summer she was going to have a tiny little Jake in her arms. Her chest constricted.

He cocked his head toward the dark pathway. "Want to head for my place?"

"Yeah. Sure." She took a trembling breath.

He linked their fingers again and led her along the grassy park beside the river. Robin was afraid to break the silence. What could have changed his mind?

Jake's front door was unlocked. Most doors in Forever didn't even have locks. In fact, most people left their keys in the vehicles. It was so different from the big city.

"Did you like the party?" he asked, dropping her shoes to the carpet in his foyer.

"Yeah," she breathed. "It was great."

"It was great," he agreed with a relaxed smile. He lifted his suit jacket off her shoulders and hung it in the closet.

"Best party I've been to in years," she said.

"Best night I've had in years." He reached around and pulled the pins out of her hair. It cascaded down and brushed her bare shoulders.

She shivered with nerves and anticipation.

He smoothed her hair out of the way and traced a line from the edge of her dress to the tip of her shoulder. "Totally and completely drop-dead gorgeous," he breathed. "Did I mention this is going to be the best night of my life?" He kissed her shoulder, starting a warm glow of desire deep in her chest.

"You want something?" he asked quietly. "Some champagne?"

Champagne? His mood worried her. He was acting as if this were a romantic date.

"I don't...think so."

He shrugged. "Okay. How about a swim in the tub?"

"Uh, Jake?"

"Hmm." He kissed her mouth, long and leisurely.

"This is...about...a baby, right?"

"Yeah." He kissed her again. "A baby." He trailed his fingertips down the exposed skin on her back. "Why? Am I doing something wrong?"

"No." No. He was doing everything so right it scared her. If she let herself, she could easily forget the goal line and submerge completely and totally into Jake's brand of seduction.

"Good." He scooped her up into his arms. "I'm willing to take all night long to make love, but if the lady wants to get down to business, we can do that, too."

His eyes shone with absolute adoration.

Unable to help herself, she trailed her fingers along his rough cheek. She leaned up and kissed his lips. His tongue responded. Sensation exploded along her limbs and her body convulsed.

He smiled, and turned for the staircase. "Have I ever told you about the beautiful young girl who nearly blew my mind one night in the Forever River?"

Thoughts of steamrollers and goal lines fled in the wake of Jake's total concentration. The only thing she was going to be able to focus on tonight was him. "No, you didn't."

"I never forgot her."

"Oh, Jake—"

"I never thought anyone could rival her. But I was wrong."

"You were?" Robin's forehead tightened in confusion and budding jealousy as Jake gently set her down in the bedroom. Was there someone else in his life?

He struck a match and lit a candle on the bedside table. "Yeah." He blew out the match. "Fifteen years later I met a woman."

He cupped Robin's face, and stared intently into her eyes. "That woman has everything I loved in the girl, and more. So much more."

Robin thought her heart was going to implode.

"Jake?"

"Hmm?" He moved her hair out of the way and kissed her neck.

"Why didn't you tell anyone?"

"Tell them what?"

"You know. That night. In the river."

"Tell them that I'd seen you naked?"

"Yeah."

"I don't rescue and tell." His voice was husky.

"I waited. I was terrified for the whole grad celebration. Sure that you'd stand up and announce it in front of the whole class." She'd sat self-consciously on that narrow, wooden chair, worrying that her skirt was too short and her neckline too low. She'd felt his intense stare the whole time, knew he was undressing her with his eyes, positive he was going to jump up and reveal all at any second.

"Why didn't you just ask me?"

"Please." She gave him a sideways smile. "I was eighteen years old. I didn't even know you."

"I knew you." He kissed her neck again, and she tipped her head to one side to give him better access. The man really was the best kisser on the planet. She could feel his hunger, feel his desire. There was something wildly erotic about being wanted so intensely by this man.

"Next time you want to know something," he whispered, "just ask me."

"Okay." No way was she going to ask him why he'd decided to make love to her. No way in the world. Gift horse in the mouth didn't quite fit here, but it was something along those lines.

"Like now," he said. "Just in case you're wondering…"

She held her breath. Maybe she wouldn't have to ask.

"What comes next? I'm about to unzip your dress."

His words sent a fresh shimmer of arousal through her. Who cared why he was doing this? She gripped his solid biceps. Just as long as he didn't change his mind.

She felt the zipper slide down. The back of the dress separated. She shifted her arms so that the dress slid off her shoulders and dropped to the floor. She stood in front of him in nothing but lacy panties and dark stockings.

Jake inhaled sharply. His hands closed on her rib cage and he covered her mouth in a hot, wide-open kiss. She curled her tongue around his. His moan vibrated through her.

He hugged her tightly. The feel of his shirt against her bare breasts sent desire pooling low in her body. She wrapped her arms around his neck and held on tight.

He broke the kiss, breathing heavily. He lifted her to lay her gently on his feather quilt. His gaze trailed along her body.

"Perfect," he whispered, hand moving to the buttons on his dress shirt.

He swiftly shucked his clothes.

"Perfect." She smiled, echoing his words, as he stretched out beside her.

He settled on his side, one arm bent and propping up his head. His fingertips trailed along her abdomen, sending licks of flame radiating in all directions. His index finger dipped into the slight indentation of her navel. Then he spread his hand out, warm palm covering her womb.

She looked into his eyes. The air suddenly thickened between them. His rough fingers flexed.

She wanted his touch. Wanted it higher, lower, everywhere. Her breasts tingled.

She moistened her lips. His gaze hungrily followed the tip of her tongue.

"Oh, Robin..." His voice was husky. His jaw was tense, though his fingers were relaxed as they trailed between her breasts, over and across her collarbone. He bent to kiss her mouth. "This is so..."

"Hard?" she asked, unable to resist the obvious joke.

He chuckled against her mouth, hand covering one of her breasts. "And how."

She quickly sobered, shifting against him, kissing him hungrily, giving her hands free license to explore his body.

He sucked in a tight breath. His calloused palm slid back down her abdomen. He slipped his hand beneath her panties. When he touched her tender flesh, she jolted, fingernails digging into his shoulders.

He pushed the final garments out of the way. Then he levered himself on top of her and settled solidly between her legs. He trapped her gaze. Passion arced between them like fork lightning. She felt moisture glisten on her skin as her throat suddenly went dry.

He went completely still for the space of several heartbeats. Then he slowly pressed into her. She shifted her hips, eyes closing as they became one.

He stilled again, leaning down to kiss her with near reverence. He tasted unbelievably sweet. Arousal built to a fever pitch as his scent surrounded her and his touch ignited her nerve endings.

"Robin?"

"Yeah?" Her voice was an octave higher than normal. This was not a particularly good time to start a conversation.

"You put all your cards on the table. It's only fair for me to do the same. I want you."

"I guessed that," she gasped.

He shifted against her, and pinpoints of light started to form on the edges of her vision.

"I want to marry you," he clarified.

"No! I can't do that. You know I won't do that." No way. No how. Not a chance. Her body was clamoring for release. Couldn't they have this argument later? She pressed her hands into the small of his back.

He didn't budge. "I think you're overreacting." He gave a wry half smile. "And I think I can change your mind."

"Fly at it, babe." She arched against him, showing him without words exactly what it was she wanted him to fly at.

He chuckled. "I was hoping you'd say that. I love you, Robin."

She froze.

Her eyes flew open.

His gorgeous, tender, loving face loomed over her. "I love you."

Her chest tightened and fear trickled through her. "No," she whispered, hot tears forming. He couldn't do that. He couldn't love her.

"It's not something I can control. It just is."

"Jake, please..." This wasn't fair. It wasn't right. She didn't want his love, couldn't handle his love.

The tears spilled from her eyes, trickling down her temples.

"Shh." He gently wiped the damp trail with his thumb. "Trust me, Robin." He slowly withdrew then plunged into her.

Her world liquefied, and she arched instinctively to meet him.

"I love you, Robin." He kissed her shoulder, stroking his tongue through the hollow formed by her collarbone. "And I promise you that I will do everything in my power to make you happy."

He thrust again, and his voice broke over his next words. "Even if it means letting you go."

Sensation rocketed through her. She wrapped herself around him, turning to kiss his hungry mouth. She'd deal with his crazy love later.

Much later.

For now, she was helpless to do anything but focus on the moment and give her passion free rein. Tomorrow could easily break her heart. But as they soared toward the pinnacle, she knew, for the moment at least, she was safe in his arms.

"ARE YOU SURE about this?" Jake sat across from Derek's custom-built russet wood desk staring at the large diamond solitaire nestled in a blue velvet box.

"Of course I'm sure." Derek looked affronted.

"I mean, this seems pretty impulsive." The Pioneer Ladies quilt jokes notwithstanding, Derek was talking married. Forever. Till death do they part. "Three days ago you were afraid to ask her to dance."

"I got over that."

"Is she that good a dancer?" Jake joked.

"Jake." Derek stood, folded his arms, and leaned back against the windowsill of his office. "There's a stunningly gorgeous, intelligent woman out there who I have respected for years. She turns me on like there's no tomorrow. She says she loves me. And she *lives* in Forever. You want me to *hesitate?*"

"Well..." When Derek put it that way, Jake did feel a little silly. He also felt more than a little jealous. Derek's dreams were coming true, while Jake's... Well, Jake's dream had left last night before her family could worry. And she had left with a decidedly dubious expression on her face. He had his work cut out for him.

"Quite frankly," said Derek, "I'm going to scoop her up before she changes her mind."

"That's what Robin said about Cindy Crawford," Jake muttered.

"What?"

"Nothing." Jake set the ring box down on the desk. "In that case, the ring is gorgeous. Congratulations. And when's the wedding?"

"Thanks," said Derek, plunking himself back down in his desk chair, a silly grin spreading across his face. "I'm going to pop the question tonight. If she's crazy enough to say yes, I'm marrying her as soon as I can."

"You have me to thank for this, you know," Jake pointed out.

"How do you figure?"

"I set you two up. At my place. The dancing."

"True enough," Derek conceded. "I guess I owe you one."

"The newspaper ad was a bust. So, yeah. You definitely still owe me one."

"Name it."

"Get Robin to stay in Forever." Even as he blurted the words, he questioned the wisdom of letting Derek in on his secret.

"You and Robin?"

Jake hesitated. But what the heck? In for a penny, in for a pound. His fingers tightened reflexively on his chair arms. "I asked her to marry me last night."

"What?" Derek rocked forward in his chair. "And you call me impulsive? You haven't even seen the woman in over fifteen years."

"She turned me down."

"Oh." Derek sat back.

Jake waved a dismissive hand. "I knew she would. She's got this great job to go back to, and she doesn't want to stay in Forever. It was a long shot, anyway."

"Have you given up?"

Jake grinned sheepishly, picking up the ring box. "Not on your life." He flipped it open and stared at the diamond and gold. "She's not leaving for another twenty-four hours." Twenty-four hours wasn't much time, but it was better than nothing. And he assumed she'd want to make love again. Just for the pregnancy effort, of course.

Derek cleared his throat. "I happen to think there's a better than even chance that Annie will ask her to be the maid of honor..."

"And..."

"That would keep her here until, say, next Saturday." Derek waggled his eyebrows. "And women get all gooey and mushy at weddings. You want to be the best man? I hear women go crazy over the best man."

"You want me to be your best man so you can fix me up with Robin?"

"It's the least I can do." Derek broke into a grin at Jake's incredulous expression. "I'm joking. I'd have asked you, anyway. But this way I get credit for a favor, too."

"Tell you what. You know the part where the best man and maid of honor sign the license?"

"Yeah."

"Switch the names so that I end up married to Robin, and we're square," Jake joked.

"What about me and Annie?"

Jake waved off Derek's concern. "She's willing. You can marry her any old time."

Derek looked heavenward and laughed. "What do you really think it would take to keep her here?"

Jake shook his head. He snapped the ring box shut again. "I don't know. A sense of a purpose, maybe. She's got this great job lined up in Toronto, lots of excitement and responsibility. I can't see her being content making crafts with the Pioneer Ladies for very long. She needs action, travel, adventure."

"Can you compromise?"

Jake tapped his fingers on the arm of the chair. "Maybe. We don't have to stay in Forever three hundred and sixty-five days a year. But there are the horses to take care of, and I want the ranch to be our home. I want our kids to go to the Forever Public School. We can't do that if she has a job in Toronto."

"What if she had a job here?"

"Doing what? She's not a carpenter. She's not a mill worker. She's not a wrangler."

"The woman has talent. You should have seen her with the Europeans."

"I did see her with the Europeans."

"That's right. You did. So you know what I mean. I could really use someone with her language and schmoozing skills to make contacts in outside markets and to entertain when the buyers come to town. Sort of a Sullivan Creations ambassador."

"Are you serious?" A buzz of excitement brewed to life in the pit of Jake's stomach. Robin with a job in Forever? An interesting and exciting world-traveling job in Forever? He tapped his fingers across his mouth to keep himself from shouting for joy. "You give her that job and we would call it *so* square."

"I'd be more than willing to make her an offer. It wouldn't be full-time, but the salary would be good and she could set her own schedule."

"You can't tell her I know about this."

"Why?"

"Well, I sort of let on that I was going to try to convince her to stay. If she thinks I put you up to it, she won't think the job is real."

"It's a real job, all right."

10

"YOUR MAID OF HONOR? You're getting married?"

At Annie's nod, Robin leaped from her chair on the back porch of her mother's house. "Oh, Annie, I'm *so* happy for you."

"So you'll do it?"

"Of course I'll do it." She immediately pulled Annie into a tight hug. Derek and Annie were going to have their happy ending. Unbidden, a tight lump formed in her chest. "Let me see the ring."

Annie held up her left hand. A large solitaire diamond sparkled in the morning sunshine.

"Gorgeous," Robin breathed. She banished a small twinge of jealousy. Jake had asked, she reminded herself. She was the one who'd said no.

"Who would have thought?" Annie grinned. "Me. Derek. I didn't think it was possible to be this happy."

"When's the wedding?" Robin's flight was leaving this afternoon, but she didn't think it would be any trouble to get some more holidays when she needed to come back.

"Friday," said Annie.

"*This* Friday?"

Annie nodded happily.

"That's only five days away." It took two days to get back to Toronto. Robin would have to turn around again after only twenty-four hours. "What's the rush?"

"No rush." Annie lowered her voice conspiratorially. "Well, actually, Derek's got this old-fashioned idea about waiting until the wedding night. And I think he's getting a little impatient."

Derek, sweet and old-fashioned? Robin was touched. Her passionate experience with Jake suddenly seemed tawdry in comparison. Though he had proposed to her before...well, *during* their lovemaking. Shouldn't that make her feel a little better?

"Can you stay for the wedding?" asked Annie.

"I'll try," Robin promised. She'd do her best. She reminded herself that this was Annie's moment, Annie's big day. Robin and Jake's relationship had nothing to do with it. She'd call Wild Ones and ask for another week of vacation.

Annie and Derek were actually getting married. Robin smiled happily at her old friend. She hugged her one more time. "This is so great."

"WELL, IT'S A BIT inconvenient, of course," said Harold Rawlings, vice-president of Wild Ones. "But I certainly understand why you want to stay. We'll just have to figure out a way to work around you. Can I fax you last week's location reports?"

Robin eagerly agreed, relieved by Harold's easy

understanding. "Sure. I'll have to find a fax number and get back to you."

"That would be helpful. Lorraine has all the files, so just give her a call when you're ready. We've got a managers' meeting on the tenth. It'll help if you're up to speed."

"No problem," said Robin. "Thanks, Harold."

"How are you enjoying that little town up there, what's it called?"

"Forever," said Robin.

"Right. Forever. Are you having a good time in Forever?"

"Yes, I am." As Robin voiced the sentiment, she realized it was true. She was having a really good time with her family and old friends. And she was glad to be staying for Annie's wedding, even looking forward to all the preparation and revelry. The citizens of Forever loved a wedding.

"Just don't get too comfortable up there. We need you back in the office."

"Don't worry." She chuckled. The novelty was fun for a week or two. But it definitely wasn't a permanent condition. "I'll be back in a week. Guaranteed."

"Good." He paused for a moment. "What's that?" His voice was muffled, as if he was talking to somebody else in the room with him.

"Lorraine says to tell you we can offer you an extra ten percent if necessary."

"Not necessary at all," Robin assured him.

"And a time-share condo in the Virgin Islands."

Robin laughed at that. "There's no need to bribe me."

"We need you back, Robin," Lorraine called into the receiver. "Soon."

"Tell her it's just a wedding," said Robin. "There are no corporate headhunters in Forever."

"She says to tell you that it's okay, as long as it's not your wedding."

Robin was forced to squelch a sudden wave of sadness. "Not mine," she said brightly. "Keep the timeshare for someone else. I'll be in the office on Monday morning."

"Enjoy the wedding," said Harold.

AT THE WEDDING REHEARSAL on Thursday night Jake was finally in the same place at the same time as Robin. To his immense frustration, she'd avoided him all week. First she and Annie were shopping for dresses, then they were choosing the flowers, then she had to host the bridal shower.

Annie managed to find time for Derek in between wedding preparations, but Robin hadn't had a single moment to spare for Jake. He didn't know how she expected to get pregnant without even being in the same room as him.

Now he and Derek stood at the front of the town church waiting for Robin, Annie, and Annie's father to emerge through the foyer entrance. In a church surrounded by people wasn't exactly how he'd been picturing her all week. But at this point, he'd take what he could get.

He shifted his stance beside Derek. Both women were dressed in casual slacks and sweaters. And they each carried a sheaf of ripened wheat, hastily picked to simulate a bouquet.

"Maid of honor first," instructed the minister from over Jake's right shoulder. "When the music comes up...okay...now."

With a last laughing comment to Annie, Robin started down the aisle. She grinned self-consciously, walking stiffly between the rows of pews. Her glance darted from the stained-glass windows to the organ pipes to the altar—everywhere but at Jake.

Halfway down the aisle, her expression sobered. Her pace smoothed to the rhythm of the touching song. Her gaze flicked to Jake and held there. She bit her bottom lip.

He was sure the flood of love and desire cascading through his system was clearly visible in his eyes. Robin walking down a church aisle toward him was a dream come true.

She, on the other hand, looked uncertain, even frightened. Her steps faltered, and for a split second he thought she was going to bolt from the church.

"Over to your left," the minister directed as she reached the front of the sanctuary. "That's right. Stop right there. Perfect."

The sheaf of wheat shook in her hands. She turned to look at Annie, her eyes shinning, blinking rapidly.

She looked so sweetly vulnerable that Jake longed to pull her into his arms.

"Bridal march comes up," said the Minister, indicating the music rise with extended arms. "Congregation stands. The bride starts down the aisle. Groom tries to look happy, not nervous."

Derek chuckled at the minister's teasing tone.

The bride and groom looked just fine. It was the maid of honor Jake was worried about. What was wrong with her? He knew women got emotional at weddings, but Robin looked completely overwhelmed by the rehearsal.

After the walk down the aisle, Annie's father took his place in the front pew and Annie handed her wheat to Robin. Her eyes narrowed in concern as she took in Robin's pale complexion and shaking hands.

"You okay?" she whispered.

Robin nodded, and offered up an almost-credible smile.

Jake took a half step toward her.

"Bride and groom face one another," the minister continued.

Robin took a deep, shuddering breath and her smile grew stronger. She nodded and motioned for Annie to continue with the rehearsal.

"Best man has the rings?" asked the minister.

"Yes," Jake affirmed.

"Best man won't forget the rings tomorrow?"

Again Derek laughed at the minister's tone.

"Best man will sleep with the rings tonight," Jake assured them all.

"Best man is ingenious," said Derek.

"Bride and groom join hands. Exchange vows. I pronounce you man and wife. You kiss."

"Can we rehearse that part?" asked Derek.

"Later," said Annie.

Jake caught Robin's gaze, but she quickly looked away. What was going on? Was she upset with him? Was she embarrassed because they'd made love? She had absolutely nothing to be embarrassed about. She was a beautiful, passionate, responsive lover.

"Then we all go up to sign the register. I'll introduce you as Mr. and Mrs. Sullivan. Congregation applauds. Maid of honor returns bouquet. Bride and groom head back down the aisle." The minister motioned to Derek and Annie.

They turned together and started walking toward the church door.

"Bride takes groom's arm," the minister called to their backs. Then he looked from Jake to Robin. "Maid of honor takes best man's arm."

Jake offered his arm to Robin. She placed her fingertips lightly in the crook of his elbow, her gaze studiously fixed on Annie's and Derek's backs. Jake could feel her hand shake. The ripened wheat heads trembled.

"You okay?" he whispered worriedly.

"Fine."

"You're shaking like a leaf."

"It's nothing."

"Robin—"

"Please, Jake."

They emerged into the foyer where Derek and Annie waited, and Jake backed off.

"That wasn't so bad," said Derek.

Robin slipped her hand from Jake's arm and retreated a few steps away. This was crazy. She was acting as if she were mad at him or something. Did she regret making love? Had she changed her mind about wanting his baby?

Well, if she had, it might very well be too late now.

"It was easy enough in blue jeans and alone," Annie warned Derek. "Just wait until tomorrow when the whole town is watching. I think I might faint."

"I'll catch you if you fall," he said. "Just don't stand me up." He draped an arm around Annie's shoulders.

"Not a chance," she responded.

Jake tried moving closer to Robin. But she shifted again, keeping the space between them constant.

"We're all done here." The minister followed them through the foyer door. "Four o'clock tomorrow afternoon. Groom arrives ten minutes early to sweat. Bride arrives two minutes late so he *really* sweats." He winked at Annie.

"Don't you dare," said Derek with mock ferocity.

Annie just laughed and patted his arm.

Derek reached out to shake the minister's hand. "We're all meeting Annie's mother in the upstairs room at the Fireweed now. Would you care to join us?"

"Thank you." The minister nodded. "That would be very nice."

POISED BESIDE THE CHURCH exit door, claustrophobia clawed at Robin's throat. At the first lull in the conversation that could possibly be interpreted as an end point, she pushed against the latch and slipped outside into the cool evening air.

She trotted down the stairs, inhaling deeply, very deeply. Then she tossed the mock bouquet over the short rectory yard fence, and broke into a run, dashing through the gate to head down the River Front Road. Her sneakers pounded against the loose gravel surface, and she raked her hands through her hair. This perfect wedding was making her teeth ache.

Annie and Derek were madly in love. Tomorrow, they'd be joined together in front of a church full of well-wishers. They'd start their perfect lives by making perfect love on their perfect wedding night.

Perfect children would come along, to be loved and cared for by both parents. Their little boys would fish with their father, their little girls would...well, probably fish with their father, too.

Robin felt like a heel for begrudging them their joy. She should be thrilled for them—flat out, no hesitation, thrilled to her toes that they were going to be so happy together.

She was the maid of honor for goodness' sake. Where had this sudden jealousy come from?

Why was it that Annie's life plan suddenly looked better than Robin's? Robin's plan was great. Her plan was perfect. She was going to have a beautiful little boy or girl who would grow up with countless opportunities right on his or her front doorstep. The nannies would be wonderful, the schools, top of the line.

She slowed to a walk, dragging deep breaths into her laboring lungs, dashing away senseless tears with the backs of her hands. If everything was going to be so perfect, why did she feel so empty?

"Robin!" came Jake's voice.

No.

Not now.

Not *now*.

She needed just a few minutes alone. If she was going to be a worthy maid of honor, if she was going to make it through dinner at the Fireweed, she had to collect herself.

She could hear his running footsteps behind her. The others would be out on the church porch by now. They'd be watching. They'd see her if she ran again.

If she didn't stop and talk to Jake, they'd assume she'd gone insane and pepper her with a million uncomfortable questions.

She dried her final tears and swallowed hard. This was Annie's big day. Robin was going to support her friend. She was going to be the best damn maid of honor in the world.

She blew out a deep breath, halted on the gravel road, and pivoted to face Jake.

"Hey," she said as he came to a stop. "I thought you'd bring your truck. I just felt like a little fresh air."

Her brilliant smile would easily fool Annie and the others who were several hundred feet away. But there was no way to hide her reddened eyes and tear trails from Jake, who was standing right in front of her.

"What is *wrong* with you?" He looked distraught.

"Nothing."

"Don't be ridiculous. You just ran away from the church."

"I wanted some fresh air."

"Talk to me, Robin."

"Remember what you said to me in the park?"

"The park?"

"Smile, talk nonsense, laugh."

"What?"

"They're coming, Jake. Let's make the dinner fun, okay?" She gently swatted Jake's arm, laughing, pretending he'd just told a joke. Then she left him standing in the middle of the road as she walked back to meet Annie.

"Whew." She pretended to wipe a sheen of sweat off her forehead. "I thought I could beat him. Guess I was wrong."

"Robin?" Annie looked concerned.

Robin linked her arm with Annie's. "Jake always could outrun me. I guess he gets the extra dessert."

She could feel Jake's penetrating gaze as he fell into step with her.

"Did you tell Derek about Connie's shower gift?" Robin prattled on, hoping no one would notice her ridiculously jovial mood swing.

"What shower gift?" Derek piped up, and Robin could have kissed him.

"You'll have to wait and see," said Annie.

"It has lace," said Robin with a wink.

"Always did like Connie," said Derek.

IN THE PRIVATE second-floor dining room of the Fireweed Café, Robin banished her melancholy mood. It wasn't the Ritz, but it was the perfect place for a happy couple to celebrate with family and friends. Candlelight shifted orange patterns on the aged pine walls, while a fireplace kept the room warm and cozy. The wide windows overlooked the river and the setting sun.

She was seated next to Jake at one end of the long rectangular table. After the waitress took their orders, everyone sipped wine, offered toasts, and shared humorous wedding stories. Robin laughed in all the right places and even added her own light anecdotes to the conversation.

While everyone's attention was focused on the minister's entertaining story about a nervous groom and the church rest room, Jake leaned toward Robin. "You doing okay?"

"Perfect." She took a quick sip of her water.

"You sure?" he asked.

"Very." She was holding her own here. She wasn't jealous of Annie anymore. She was happy for her.

Jake reached beneath the tablecloth and captured her hand where it rested in her lap. His work-roughened thumb stroked her palm. "Are you having second thoughts?"

His light touch evoked vivid memories of their single night together. Well, their half night together. Okay, their two hours together.

She'd missed his touch the past few days. She'd missed him. She'd missed the amazing magic they made together.

Their lovemaking hadn't been tawdry. It just hadn't been... Legal? Sanctioned? Married?

Why was she obsessing about this?

"Second thoughts about what?" she whispered, forcing herself to tug her hand away.

"Having my baby?"

"No. *No!*" She quickly glanced at the other diners to see if they were paying any attention. They weren't.

"So why haven't we made love again?"

"Jake. Not here."

"I haven't seen you all week. You couldn't wait to get me into bed the first time. What happened?"

Excellent question. Robin knew darn well her

chances of conceiving were better if they made love two or three nights in a row. Why hadn't she done that?

Jake's ludicrous threat to marry her was a non-issue. She'd no more marry him and move to Forever than she'd fly to the moon. Which, although comforting, didn't answer the question of why she hadn't made love with him again.

Was it because he'd said he loved her?

"Robin?"

The man sitting next to her loved her. An unbidden glow of happiness surged through her body. Really *loved* her?

How did he know?

How could he tell?

"Robin, are you upset?"

"Just emotional." She took another swallow of her water. She wished she could take a bracing swig of wine, but liquor was off her list for the next while. "Weddings are very moving events."

"Yeah. They are." His voice dropped to the husky, passionate timbre she remembered so well. "Want to have one?"

Her heart lurched to her throat. She shot him a scowl. "That was unfair."

"All's fair in love and war, babe," he said mildly.

"Which is this?" she asked while the other diners' conversations continued to flow around them.

"That's up to you. Do you want to love me or fight with me?"

"Neither." Her fingers tightened on the water glass.

"You just want my baby."

"Right."

"What do you figure the odds on that are?" he asked.

"The odds?"

"The odds that you're pregnant. Since we only made love once."

"Do we *need* to have this conversation now?"

"Want to meet me later? My place?"

Her stomach clenched. His place? Just the two of them? With him talking of love and marriage. Red flags popped up in front of her and warning sirens sounded in her brain. "No."

"Then we have it now."

"Eighty-five percent."

"Don't be sarcastic." He lifted his wineglass and took a quick sip.

"It's true."

"You can't be that precise."

"I read a book on conception. I have a thermometer."

He stared at her in silent confusion, wineglass still poised next to his cheek.

"A woman's temperature rises slightly when she's fertile."

"Really?"

"Really."

"And yours was..."

"Up." She nodded decisively.

"Oh." He grew silent.

WHILE THE OTHERS LINGERED over coffee, Robin stood by the picture window and watched lightning flash above the faraway mountains. Eighty-five percent. That was the statistical chance that she had conceived that night with Jake. Her hand rose to her abdomen. She didn't feel pregnant.

She wondered what pregnant felt like.

"Robin?" Derek stepped up beside her at the window.

"Hi, Derek." She smiled, and let her hand drop. "Great dinner."

"Glad you enjoyed it. You okay?"

She nodded. "I'm great. I'll probably bawl my eyes out tomorrow though." She laughed lightly.

He smiled in return, then focused on the faraway storm clouds. "Before I get too busy and forget, there's something I wanted to discuss with you."

Curious, Robin gazed at his profile. "There is?"

He nodded, one hand coming up to rub his chin. "Mmm-hmm."

"Okay?" She couldn't imagine what Derek would need to discuss with her on the eve of his wedding.

"The van der Pols were very impressed with you."

She smiled. "Thanks. I liked them, too. Are they going to sell your furniture in Holland?"

"There's a good chance that they will."

"That's great."

"I have some other European buyers coming over in a couple of weeks. I have someone in about once a month through most of the year. I also need to visit foreign markets with some regularity."

"That's nice." Robin was glad to hear that his business was doing well. Though it hardly seemed important enough to discuss at his rehearsal dinner.

He cleared his throat. "I need help with that, Robin. I need somebody who can fit in with other cultures when necessary. Who can undertake corporate entertaining on occasion. And who can translate for me when the need arises."

"Makes sense." Thunder rolled in the distance in front of them and the murmur of conversation and laughter filled the room behind.

"I need *you*, Robin." He continued staring out the window.

"What?" She blinked in confusion.

"You. I think you're the right person for the job."

"What job?"

"The ambassadorial position with Sullivan Creations."

She shook her head and peered closely at Derek. "You're offering me a job?"

"Yeah." He looked directly at her for the first time. "That's what I've been talking about."

"Wait a minute. Why would you do this?"

"Like I said, the van der Pols—"

She waved her hand dismissively. "Yeah, yeah. The van der Pols liked me. But you know I'm not—"

Her eyes widened and her stomach plummeted. "Did Jake put you up to this?"

Derek glanced away.

"Derek!" Her gaze shot to where Jake was chatting with Annie's mom and the minister.

"Okay, okay. Jake knows." He looked back at her, bald sincerity in his eyes. "But the job's real."

"How could you?"

"You don't have to decide right away."

"I'm not staying, Derek. I don't care what kind of a high-salary, fluff position you and Jake dreamed up. I'm *not* staying in Forever. Got that?"

"Like I said, Robin." He looked as if he was hiding a smile. "You don't have to answer right away."

"No."

"Just think about it."

"No."

"For a day or two."

"No."

"You can let me know next week." With a relieved smile, he turned to walk back to the other guests.

Robin gripped the cold windowsill. Now that was a classic what-part-of-no-don't-you-understand moment.

She nearly laughed at the irony. Just when she'd told Harold that there were no headhunters in Forever.

There was a headhunter here, all right. His name was Jacob Bronson.

11

JAKE SEATED Annie's mother in the front pew and handed her one of the clean cloth hankies that he'd loaded in his tux pockets prior to the ceremony. He figured Robin and Annie's mother were both sure things. But he was also giving long odds on both Eunice and Alma May.

Their eyes were suspiciously bright as they glanced around the decorated church and spoke in low tones to one another. Weddings and babies. Both sent the Forever ladies into outbursts of either squeals or tears. Jake was willing to bet that their cheeks would be soaked already if Robin was in the wedding dress.

He watched them thoughtfully. Robin in a wedding dress. How were they going to react if Robin showed up with a baby next year? How would they feel about skipping the wedding and going directly to a grandchild?

How would they react when they found out he'd fathered that child? He swallowed, suddenly feeling as though he'd betrayed their trust. He'd slept with their baby girl. He might have made her pregnant without marrying her.

Alma May caught his gaze and smiled. Guilt suddenly gripped his gut.

They'd be furious with him, and rightly so. At best, they'd be disappointed in him.

And what about Robin? They were so proud of the little girl who'd gone out into the world and made good. How would they feel about her indiscretion?

Sure, women had babies out of wedlock all the time nowadays. But Eunice and Alma May were from a different era. More so because they'd spent their entire lives in Forever.

They'd be upset, hurt, disappointed. Jake wouldn't hurt Eunice and Alma May for the world. And he wouldn't hurt Robin. Nor would he allow Robin to hurt herself.

Not when he could put a stop to it.

His gaze strayed down the aisle. He could see Robin and Annie making final preparations in the foyer. Seating the mother of the bride was Jake's last duty before the wedding began, and it was almost time for him to take his place at the front with Derek.

He took a bracing breath. With solid determination, he left his appointed spot and strode to the back of the church. Robin was brushing the final wrinkles out of Annie's dress.

"Jake?" She started, straightening quickly as she spotted him. "You're not supposed to be here."

The organist changed songs, and Jake glanced at his watch. T minus two minutes, and counting.

"I have to talk to you." He cupped Robin's elbow, attempting to pull her away from Annie.

"Now?" Robin didn't budge.

"Now?" Annie echoed.

"I am *so* sorry, Annie. Please believe me, I wouldn't do this if I thought I had a choice."

"What's wrong, Jake?" Robin's eyes widened.

"I was just watching your grandmother."

"Why? Is she sick?" Robin quickly craned her neck to see into the church.

"No. No, Robin, she's fine. She's just fine." Well, that was a brilliant move. Scare the heck out of her and then propose. He regrouped and tried again. "Did you see how happy she is about Annie's wedding?"

"Uh-huh." Robin cautiously nodded, glancing at Annie with an expression that clearly said she thought Jake had lost his mind. Well, maybe he had.

"Have you ever considered how she'd feel about your wedding?"

The nodding abruptly ceased. Robin's eyes widened. Then anger flashed in their depths. "Jake! I *cannot* believe you're doing this—"

"Robin—"

"Maybe all's fair when it comes to you and me—"

"Robin—"

"But this is Annie's day. Derek's day. You get back up to the front of the church—"

"I'm sorry, Annie." Jake interjected another apology. He only had one minute left. Time was running out, and he had to make Robin understand. "Have you stopped to consider what you're doing to your family?"

"Yes," she hissed. "Yes, yes, and *yes*."

"I don't think you have."

"I don't care what you think."

Jake took a deep breath. "Robin," he said in a reasonable tone. "If you show up next summer with my baby in your arms—"

Annie gasped.

"—I want that baby to have my name. I want *you* to have my name."

"Baby?" asked Annie in a strangled voice. The organist started the final song before the bridal procession.

"I won't do it," said Robin.

"Please," said Jake, alarm inching its way into his system. "For your mom. For your grandmother. Marry me now. We'll figure out the rest later."

"Jake. I'm leaving." Her words had a disheartening ring of finality. This wasn't going to work. He wasn't going to convince her. He was going to fail, damn it.

"I know you have a plane ticket," he rushed on. "Do whatever you have to do tomorrow. But marry me now. Spend our wedding night with me. Then, when—*if* you come back with my baby, your grandmother and mother won't be disappointed in you. Disappointed in *me*. Do it for them, Robin."

Annie's shocked gaze moved swiftly from Robin to Jake and back again.

"I'm sorry, Annie," Jake repeated for the third time. "Would you mind? Would Derek mind?"

"Sharing our wedding?"

"Yeah."

"No." Annie shook her head. She reached out and grabbed both of Robin's hands. "Do it, Robin."

Robin stared blankly at Annie. She looked stunned, shell-shocked.

"We have a church full of friends and family," said Jake. "A minister. Flowers. You even have a bouquet." He gestured in almost-comic desperation to the yellow roses in her hand. "I love you, Robin. But I swear I'll let you go."

Robin opened her mouth, closed it, then opened it again. The minister was heading down the aisle toward them, and Annie's father was crossing the foyer.

"Get married, Robin," said Annie, her eyes shining. "A baby. My goodness. You and Jake? This is wonderful."

"Please, Robin," said Jake.

The minister bustled through the doorway. "We have to get started."

"Robin?" asked Jake.

Annie nodded vigorously, all smiles. She squeezed Robin's hands.

"Jake," said the minister. "We really have to..." He gestured toward the front of the church where Derek was probably panicking by now.

Jake stared at Robin. He put all the love and honesty he could muster into his silent plea.

She gave a small nod.

His heart leaped. "Yeah?"

She nodded again.

Jake turned to the minister. "Can you do two weddings?"

The minister looked at him blankly.

"Two?" asked Annie's father.

"WHERE HAVE YOU BEEN?" Derek frantically whispered as Jake took his place at the front of the sanctuary. "I thought I was being stood up by both the bride and the best man."

Jake stifled a laugh.

Derek straightened his collar. "It was starting to look like the two of you ran off together."

"Is that what you thought?" asked Jake. He was having a hard time keeping the euphoria out of his voice. He felt as though he'd pulled off the coup of the century. He couldn't even find it in him to care that after tonight his and Robin's marriage might very well be nothing but two names on a piece of paper.

"No." Derek cleared his throat. "Of course not."

"Sorry I worried you."

"*I* wasn't worried. Everyone else was. What happened?"

"Robin and I are getting married," said Jake with a short sigh of satisfaction.

Derek's eyes widened. "Really? When?"

"Now."

"What do you mean, now?"

The minister breezed past in his dark flowing robe, momentarily distracting them both. He took his place in front of the altar, and the organist immediately struck up the wedding march.

"What do you mean, now?" Derek asked as he and Jake spun around to face the back of the church.

"I mean right now."

Robin and Annie started down the aisle, one on each of Annie's father's arms.

"Hope you don't mind." Though, frankly, Jake was too exhilarated to care much whether Derek minded or not.

"I don't mind at all," Derek deadpanned. "Who wouldn't want to have his wedding hijacked by the guy who almost ran off with his bride?"

"I brought my own bride," Jake corrected with a grin.

"You definitely owe me one," said Derek.

The minister cleared his throat behind them, and Jake zipped his lip, focusing his attention on Robin as she continued down the aisle. Though her dress was simpler than Annie's, her bouquet smaller, and she had tiny flowers woven into her hair instead of a veil, she easily outshone every woman in the room.

"Isn't she gorgeous?" Derek whispered, clearly in awe of Annie in her layers of lace and chiffon.

"Sure is," answered Jake, eyes riveted on Robin's elegant dress of ivory and forest-green.

The two brides came to a stop at the front of the church to the unabashed curiosity of the congregation.

"Ladies and gentlemen," the minister began. "We are blessed today with not one, but two brides."

There were gasps and murmurs throughout the church as Annie's father stepped back out of the way. Jake quickly captured Robin's cold hands. Her lips and cheeks were pale. He surreptitiously rubbed her fingers and held her gaze, trying to get her to relax, trying to coax a smile.

This was a good thing they were doing, making sure their child was legitimate.

Eunice stood up from her second-row pew. She quickly moved forward to wrap Robin in a tearful hug. She kissed her daughter's cheek and cradled her face in her hands. Her eyes glowed with happiness.

She took half a step back and placed a shaking hand over her chest. Then she glanced from Robin to Jake and back again, letting out a weak laugh. An obvious veteran of many weddings, she quickly collected herself and relieved both Robin and Annie of their bouquets before taking her place in the pew.

Robin turned her attention to Jake. Her eyes filled, and she started to tremble. He pulled her closer, passing her one of his cloth hankies.

"Dearly Beloved..." the minister began.

THE MINISTER'S droning voice, the scent of melted wax, and the blur of old, familiar faces swirled around Robin, making her feel as though she'd crossed to another dimension. She kept expecting to wake up.

This could be a dream.

It *must* be a dream.

But the hands that engulfed hers were warm and strong, and frighteningly real. And Jake's smile looked more than physical. His lips were firm and inviting, and his eyes crinkled in the corners the way that she loved.

If this wasn't a dream, it was definitely the craziest thing she'd ever done—and that was saying quite a lot, given the bungee jump.

She squeezed his hands experimentally. Yep, they were real enough.

He squeezed back, conveying the silent message that everything was going to be okay. She had no idea why, but she suddenly believed him. In the midst of a surreal experience, he was her anchor. Just as he'd been that night fifteen years ago.

This was the boy who had walked away and remained silent to protect her. The man who had saved her life, rocked her in his arms and declared his love. The man who cared so much about her family and his unborn child that he was willing to marry her to protect them. Even though he knew the marriage would never be real. Even though he knew she would leave him tomorrow.

His hands tightened on hers once more. "I love you," he mouthed.

Her lips parted, and a powerful wave of emotion rocked her world. Because she'd almost said the words back.

She'd almost told him that she loved him. Because she did. She loved him.

She loved Jake.

"Jake?" said the minister. "Will you take Robin to be your lawfully wedded wife?"

"Yes," Jake whispered, voice husky, gaze never leaving hers. "I will."

A lone tear clung to her lower lash for a second before sliding down her cheek. Her chest swelled. Her knees went weak.

"And, Robin," said the minister. "Will you take Jake to be your lawfully wedded husband?"

"I will." Her voice was barely audible, barely recognizable.

"The rings," said the minister.

Jake quickly pulled out the matched set of gold and diamond bands for Annie and Derek. Then a look of distress crossed his face when he realized he didn't have a ring for Robin.

Someone rustled in a pew behind them. A murmur started throughout the church. Jake glanced up, confusion obvious on his face. Robin turned in time to see her grandmother stand up in the aisle.

With a warm smile, Alma May walked toward them. She gently wiped the tear trail from Robin's face. "I always knew you'd find your way home," she said, her voice husky with age and emotion.

She turned to Jake, and with slow deliberation, for the first time in over fifty years, removed the raw gold nugget wedding band from her ring finger.

Robin's chest constricted. She shook her head no, but words wouldn't come.

Jake put his hand over Alma May's, stopping her.

She smiled at Jake, and a tear glistened in her ageless eyes. "It's our gift," she said. "These were the first nuggets discovered in Forever. They started the town. Then they brought me here. But now they have another job to do."

She placed the old ring in Jake's hand with a regal nod. Then she slowly returned to her seat.

Jake swallowed, looking completely stunned.

Robin stared at the small ring in his palm. She'd heard the story a hundred times. Her grandfather had found the small nuggets in a creek just north of Forever, starting the mini gold rush that created the town. He'd had them set in a wedding band to prove to Alma May's parents that he was a man of means.

At the time, they represented all of his worldly wealth. But before Alma May realized he wasn't rich, they were already married and Eunice was on the way. In love with her new husband, she'd defied her family's wishes and stayed.

"Shall we continue?" asked the minister.

THE GOLD NUGGET RING glittered on Robin's finger as Jake scooped her into his arms and carried her across the threshold of his front door. The town hotel didn't offer anything as fancy as a honeymoon suite. Besides, he wanted to hold Robin all night long in his own bed.

He wasn't sure what to do about Alma May's gift. There was no way to give it back without exposing the marriage as a sham, but Jake didn't want to keep it under false pretences, either.

As he lowered Robin to the floor, he touched the rough gold, warm from her skin.

"Jake—" she began.

"Shh," he admonished.

"This is all so—"

He put a finger over her lips. "For tonight," he said, "you are my bride."

"But—" Her protest was muffled by his fingertip.

"Just for tonight," he repeated with a small shake of his head. "That's all I ask."

Her blue-green eyes hesitated, the war behind them plain for him to see. Then she nodded. And he smiled.

"Kiss me, husband," she whispered.

He did.

He carried her to his room. He made love to her on the land that his grandfather had tilled, blessed by the ring her grandfather had forged. Gently, at first, but with increasing fervor and urgency as the moon galloped across the sky toward morning.

In the predawn darkness, he held her tightly and

fought the loss of consciousness that would take her from him.

"I love you," she whispered.

And then he knew the ring wouldn't be wasted. And he knew he could finally sleep. His lashes gave way to the irresistible force pressing them down.

SHE LOVED HIM. Robin clasped a trembling hand over her mouth, backing away from the bed where Jake slept soundly.

The backs of her knees hit the rocking chair and gave way. She sat down hard.

Something had gone terribly wrong in the two weeks since she'd come to visit Forever. It was a form of insanity. Or maybe some kind of hypnosis.

Fate?

If this was what happened when you let fate take the driver's seat, Robin was never doing it again. She'd almost lost her life, almost lost everything she'd worked toward for the past decade and a half.

When she'd arrived in Forever, she'd wanted nothing more than to celebrate with her family and get back on the plane to start her new and perfect life. Then she'd met Jake again. Then she'd made love with Jake. Then she'd...she swallowed...married Jake.

And now.

Now, she was in *love* with Jake. And, heaven help her, she wanted to stay. She actually wanted to chuck her other life and crawl back into bed with her new husband and lay in his arms as long as he was willing to hold her.

She shook her head. Terror constricted her heart as she began jerkily rocking the chair.

If she didn't get the heck out of town in the next few hours, she was going to be trapped. She'd never escape.

He shifted in the bed, one arm reaching out as if seeking her. She froze in mid-rock. He frowned in his sleep.

Then his breathing evened out, and she dared to stand up.

It was now or never.

Quickly gathering her bridesmaid dress, underwear and stockings, she tiptoed to the bedroom door.

Unable to make it any further, she stopped, gripping the handle as her heart tore in two. She stared at Jake, sprawled across the big bed, one arm flung across her pillow, shoulders and biceps solid even in sleep. She could still smell his scent on her body, still feel his fingertips exploring, arousing, worshiping, still taste his frantic kisses.

A sob escaped and she quickly clasped a hand over her mouth, afraid she would wake him.

She didn't want to wake him.

Did she?

For a crazy second she found herself hoping he'd wake up, hoping he'd stop her, hoping he'd pin her with that sexy half smile that would most certainly make her stay—at least another hour, maybe even long enough to miss her plane.

She stopped breathing, heart thudding, waiting...watching.

Then she closed her eyes to block him from view, reaching deep inside herself for the strength she needed to move.

Focus. Goal line. Steamroller.

She *had* to do this.

With her eyes shut tight, she whispered, "Goodbye," blew him a tender kiss, and slipped through the doorway.

TWO HOURS LATER, in the gray light of dawn, the Beaver floatplane warmed up beside the dock. The air was chilly on Robin's bare arms, the streets deserted.

If the pilot found anything odd about a woman standing on the dock in evening wear with nothing but a small purse in her hand, he didn't mention it. She had a ticket, and he had a schedule.

She compulsively pushed her grandmother's ring around and around in circles on her finger. There was no gracious way to give it back. And Jake was right. It was better for her family and their possible child if people thought they were married.

He'd have to make up a story about why she left town as planned. She could trust him to do that. She could trust him with anything.

Except her heart. She instinctively placed a hand

over her chest. She couldn't let him trap her heart. He'd sworn to let her go, he'd sworn—

"We're ready, ma'am." The pilot's voice startled her. The passenger door squeaked gently as he opened it. Robin squared her shoulders.

As she turned to board the plane, a small movement caught her eye. She squinted through the gloom to the end of the dock.

Her heart plummeted.

Jake.

She had no idea how long he'd been standing there, shirt unbuttoned, faded jeans riding low on his hips.

The sun peeked over the horizon, silhouetting him in an orange glow. He straightened his shoulders. His air of defeat turned to one of condemnation as their gazes met and locked. His eyes were flints in a stony mask.

He was furious.

You promised! she wanted to yell. But her face was frozen, her vocal chords inoperable.

For a split second he rocked forward on the balls of his feet. She held her breath and waited, but he didn't move.

He'd promised to let her go. And she had to leave. It was that simple.

"Ma'am?" prompted the pilot.

Robin turned toward the airplane, nodded stiffly, and swung up onto the narrow step.

There was nothing left to say.

12

"WANT TO JOIN US for a drink?" Lorraine stuck her head into Robin's office at five o'clock. Her colleague was a tall, willowy redhead, who always radiated energy and exuberance.

Robin's first instinct was to say no. The last thing she felt like doing tonight was sitting through the loud music and hearty laughter of the Top Hat Bar. But then she realized that she'd said no to Lorraine's last two invitations.

In the three weeks since she'd returned from Forever, she'd been aloof to the point of rudeness. Camaraderie was an important component of Wild Ones's management team philosophy. She needed to get back on amicable footing with the other managers.

"Sure." She forced a smile. "I just need about half an hour to finish compiling this presentation—"

"Forget the presentation," said Lorraine. "I'll let you in on a secret. We waived your six-month probation period, you don't have to kill yourself to impress us."

Robin chuckled self-consciously. She had been a bit eager since starting the new job. Lorraine had obviously chalked it up to overzealousness. The truth was, working hard left her with little time to think.

"Meet us downstairs in five." Lorraine didn't give her time to argue as she headed back toward her own office.

It didn't take a psychiatrist to tell Robin she was using work as a panacea for depression and loneliness. And it worked fine during the days, and even during the evenings. It was the nights that were doing her in.

Every time she closed her eyes she saw Jake's face. At times she saw his anger when she confessed her plan to get pregnant. Then she saw his tenderness when he rescued her from the river. She saw his joy at their wedding ceremony, and even his passion on their wedding night. But the image that intruded most often, the one that kept her from getting more than a few hours' sleep each night, was his desolation as he'd watched her on the dock.

Before he'd masked it with anger, for a split second, his raw pain had been exposed for her to see. It had touched her to the core, because she'd recognized it as her own.

She punched the Off button on her computer terminal. She had to forget it. To survive, she had to forget him.

"Let's go, Robin," Lorraine called cheerfully through the open door. She stood with her purse and coat in her hand.

"On my way." Robin retrieved her own purse from

the bottom drawer of her desk and shrugged into her blazer.

Tonight she was forgetting. Tonight she was joining her co-workers at the Top Hat Bar. She wouldn't drink alcohol, since tomorrow was the first day a home pregnancy test would be accurate. But she was going to have a great time all the same.

Maybe she'd come home so exhausted from joking and laughing and talking that she'd fall into a dead sleep. Maybe Jake wouldn't intrude on her dreams. Maybe she'd be able to convince herself that her perfect job and her perfect life were going to turn out perfectly, after all.

SLEEP DIDN'T QUITE turn out the way she'd planned.

By 5:00 a.m., she sat on her bathroom counter, bare legs bent, heels resting against the edge of the sink, back to the wall, reading the home pregnancy test instructions for the third time. It looked simple enough. There was really no reason to go over them with a fine-tooth comb, certainly no reason to read them in three of the four different languages.

If she was pregnant in English, she'd most definitely be pregnant in French, too. She was stalling. She was simply terrified to find out.

She wanted Jake's baby, wanted his baby so bad her heart ached with it. If she wasn't pregnant now, she was under no illusion that she could go back to try again. She doubted he'd make love to her now.

And if he did, she doubted he'd let her go a second time.

Who was she kidding?

She wouldn't be able to walk away from him a second time if her life depended on it.

She gritted her teeth and hopped down. She was either pregnant or she wasn't. Sitting on the cold countertop, reading a Spanish description of a blue stripe, wasn't going to change that fact one way or the other.

She carefully followed the instructions, then forced herself to leave the room while the prescribed three minutes ticked by.

She headed into her small study and booted up her computer.

One minute gone.

She opened her e-mail. There were twenty-five new messages. None of which looked urgent. None of which she could concentrate on in any event.

Two minutes gone.

She straightened the stack of bills beside her monitor, then picked up her water glass and walked toward the bathroom.

Twenty seconds early, she stopped outside the door and closed her eyes, counting one steamboat, two steamboats, all the way up to twenty-five just to be sure.

Then she stepped into the room, and focused on the plastic container.

Blue stripe.

She picked it up.

Definitely a blue stripe.

She compared her results to the drawing on the little instruction booklet.

Yep. It was positive. She was pregnant.

Her hands started to shake and she quickly set the test back down on the counter. A wave of disbelief coursed over her as she continued to stare at the plastic container. She was going to have Jake's baby. They'd really done it.

Joy surged through her. She clasped her hands to her abdomen and grinned at her reflection in the mirror.

She had to do something to celebrate. She had to tell somebody. She had to tell Jake.

Her expression sobered.

She wanted to tell *Jake*.

Of all the people in the world, Jake was the one she wanted to phone at a ridiculously early hour in the morning and share the news. He was going to be a father. Well, an absent father.

Some of her joy evaporated.

She couldn't share the news with Jake. It didn't affect his life. He might not even be happy about it. She certainly wouldn't be happy to know that she was going to be a parent who rarely saw her child. She'd be downright distraught.

Still, he was the one she wanted to share it with. And he certainly had a right to know.

Maybe he wouldn't be angry.

Maybe he'd come to terms with her leaving.

Maybe his heart had healed a whole lot better than hers. Because all she'd thought about since leaving him behind was how much she loved him, and how much she missed him, and how Toronto seemed lonely and impersonal compared to the casual familiarity of Forever.

She forced those thoughts away. She was here. She was pregnant. And she was happy about it. Life was going to be so perfect from here on in.

Still, maybe she should give him a quick call. Just to let him know the news. Just to hear the sound of his voice.

She wandered into the bedroom, sat on the bed, and stared at the phone.

He'd probably like to know one way or the other.

He was probably wondering.

She really owed it to him.

She reached for the receiver.

She dialed the area code and the first three digits of his number before slamming the receiver back down on its cradle. She bit her lip, took a deep breath, and closed her eyes. She could do this.

She picked up the receiver and punched in his number.

The ringer buzzed in her ear. She gripped the handset tightly, trying to resist the urge to hang up before he answered.

"Hello?" His voice was half sharp with adrenaline, half groggy with sleep. Too late, she remembered the time zone difference.

"Jake?" Her voice was little more than a croak.

"Robin?"

"Yeah. It's me."

"What's going on?"

She could hear his covers rustle. Pictured him sitting up, his feet shifting over the side of the bed, his glance at his alarm clock, his fingers running through his tousled hair.

"Robin?" he breathed. "Are you there?"

"I'm here."

"What time is it there? Is everything okay?"

"It's morning here," she answered. "Barely. I...uh..." Now that she had him on the line, she didn't know what to say. This wasn't exactly the kind of thing you just blurted out from three thousand miles away.

The seconds ticked off. She considered asking about the weather, but that would be ridiculous. He'd probably already guessed the single reason she would call him at this hour.

"I'm pregnant," she blurted, ending her own suspense as much as his.

He didn't respond. She couldn't even hear him breathing.

"Jake?"

"Yeah?" Short. Clipped. Furious.

"I'm..."

"Is that all?" he asked, his voice stone-cold.

She cleared her throat. "Yeah. I guess that's it." A single taste of his voice and her heart was breaking all over again. Her life plan had seemed so sound and logical when she first came up with it. But she'd taken a wrong turn somewhere, made some kind of terrible miscalculation, because she was miserable without him.

How had it come to this? How had she ended up wanting nothing more than to stay on the phone with an angry Jake? Why was it his voice that made her feel alive, his voice that banished the loneliness?

She wanted him back. She wanted it all. She wanted his face, his warmth, his love.

Him.

Nothing but him.

"Well, thanks," he said in that same cold voice.

"No problem," she whispered, swallowing painfully, desperately holding back tears. Life was never going to be okay again.

"Goodbye, Robin." His hang-up clicked in her ear before she had a chance to beg.

JAKE STARED AT THE PHONE in his moonlit bedroom, frustration seething within him. He'd behaved like a jerk, he knew. But the woman was ripping out his heart and soul.

How dare she be pregnant?

How dare she call him to tell him?

How dare she set his recovery back to square one?

He slumped down, elbows on his knees. When he'd promised to let her go, he'd been certain it wouldn't come to that. He'd been certain there was a fixed quotient of pain in every man's life, and her leaving would put him way over the maximum.

And then when she'd told him she loved him, he thought he was home free. His mistake, he knew now. The Ice Princess wouldn't let something as trivial as love get in the way of her precious independent life.

Still. Just now, he'd behaved like a jerk.

His hands knotted into fists.

He had to fix this. For better or worse, she was his wife. She was having his child. No matter how far estranged, they were his family, and he didn't have the luxury of hurting them because he was angry.

Somehow, some way, he had to fix this.

He grabbed the phone and punched in Derek's number.

Derek answered on the first ring. "Yeah?"

"It's Jake."

There was a momentary pause. "What's up?"

"I need to get to Toronto."

"What?" Then Derek's voice dropped to a stage whisper. "It's Jake. It's late, honey. Go back to sleep. Toronto?" He was back with Jake again.

"Robin's pregnant."

"Really?" His voice grew muffled again. "Robin. She's pregnant."

"I need to get down there." Jake rubbed his hand along the tight corded muscles at the back of his neck.

"Right," said Derek. "Grab a floatplane as soon as

it's light. I'll have the jet meet you at the Whitehorse Airport."

Jake dropped his hand back to the bed in relief. He was already formulating a world record escape plan. He'd get his top wrangler to move in and take care of the horses. He had no idea how long he'd be gone.

If there was an answer to this, he was going to find it. And the answer sure as hell wasn't having him and Robin on opposite sides of the country.

"I owe you big-time," he said to Derek.

"You bet you owe me, buddy. What?" Derek's voice became muffled again. He chuckled. "Annie says, you make Robin happy, and she'll pay your debt in full... Huh...? How...? Oh, *babe*... Gotta go, Jake. You don't owe me a thing."

Derek hung up the phone.

JAKE SAT ON THE FLOOR outside Robin's apartment, counting the gold swirls on the hallway wallpaper pattern and wondering how she'd react to seeing him.

He should have called back this morning and warned her he was coming. He drummed his fingers against his knee. But she might have refused to see him. Even now, she might refuse to speak to him.

He'd hurt her on the phone. She'd called to share the news of a lifetime, and he'd hurt her. He didn't know what he'd do if she turned him away.

The elevator door slid open, and he jumped to his

feet. He cocked his head to one side, pulse pounding, waiting for the passengers to exit.

Robin. Finally.

His heart soared at the sight of her. Fatigue and worry slipped from his shoulders. She was here, and for the moment that was all that mattered. He couldn't stop the stupid grin that covered his face at the sight of her.

When she spotted him, her footsteps faltered on the thick hallway carpet.

"Jake?" She squinted in disbelief.

"Hi, Robin." He had to restrain himself from rushing over to pull her into his arms.

"But..." She motioned in the general direction of north. "This morning...Jake, how did you get here?"

"A jet," he answered, taking an involuntary step forward.

"That's impossible. It takes two days—"

"I took Derek's Learjet. Come here."

"But—"

"Come here, Robin." He forced a light note into his voice, amazed it wasn't shaking. "I've traveled four thousand miles. The least you can do is kiss me hello."

She didn't fall for it. She didn't move. "I don't understand."

He moved boldly toward her. His voice dropped and slowed. "I promised I'd let you go." He halted in front of her, staring down in to her beautiful, bottomless eyes. "I never promised I wouldn't follow you."

"Oh, Jake." Tears gathered on her lashes.

He reached forward and brushed a curl off her forehead. "I don't know where we go from here, sweetheart. But you and me have *got* to find a way to be together."

"Jake, I'm sorry." Her voice caught on the words, and her trembling hand flew to her mouth.

"Shh." He pulled her into his arms, rocking her rhythmically. Finally.

"I was wrong." Her tear-filled words were muffled against his chest. "I thought I could do it," she whispered. "But I couldn't."

Jake froze.

"I just couldn't go through with it."

Couldn't go through with what? Loving him? Having his baby? Was she contemplating something unthinkable?

"What do you mean?" he rasped.

"I'm so..." She unsuccessfully fought back a sob. "Robin—"

"I thought it was the best thing—"

"Robin!" he stepped back, holding her away from him.

"I truly didn't mean for anyone—"

"You're scaring me." Was he overreacting? Would she really consider ending the pregnancy?

"I've been scaring myself."

"What are you talking about? Why are you sorry?" He desperately needed an explanation.

"I never meant to hurt you."

"I'm fine." Yeah, okay, he was in agony without her. But that didn't mean he didn't want this baby. Whether he raised it or not, he *wanted* this baby.

"I'm not fine." Her voice shook. "I'm throwing it all away. I'm giving it all up. I want to come home."

"Home?" She'd lost him with that one.

"Home. To Forever. To you." Her breath shuddered. "Oh, Jake. I was so wrong."

Jake blinked, numbed by her words. She was coming home?

"The baby?" he asked.

She gave a watery laugh. "Well, if I come home, it's a given the baby comes, too."

She was bringing his baby home? "Are you saying...?"

"Do you still want me?" Her hesitancy touched him to the core. Still want her? What a question.

"Yes," he rasped.

"I love you, Jake."

"I know." He blew out a breath, hugging her close, tight, so tight. "I just never thought it would be enough."

"It's enough. It's more than enough."

"Oh, Robin." His body convulsed as he lifted her from the ground, burying his face in her neck.

She sighed and tucked her cheek against his shoulder, fingers exploring his hair and face for long minutes as if she wanted to memorize him.

She hiccuped. Then she pulled back and smiled. "What's this about Derek and a plane?"

"Derek's dad has a jet." He slowly lowered her to the floor, giving in to the impulse to lay his hand on her flat abdomen. It felt as if the earth shifted beneath him.

"Who's Derek's dad?"

"Roland Sullivan." Jake absently supplied the name of the prominent West Coast industrialist. "There's really a baby in here?"

Her eyes widened. "Derek is Roland Sullivan's son?"

"Yes. How do you feel? Are you sick?"

"I'm fine. Then Derek must be—"

"Rich?" Jake pressed his thumb gently over her navel.

"Yeah." She sighed and covered his hand with her smaller one.

"Definitely."

"So why does he live in—"

"Robin." Jake peered down at her in mock reproach. "When will you get it through your head that only the very best people live in Forever?"

She grinned. "Sorry."

"And well you should be. Got a key to this place?"

"Yes." She unzipped her purse and dug her hand inside. "I can't believe you're here."

"I'm here." He reluctantly let go of her while she twisted the key in the lock.

She opened the door and turned on the lights. The apartment was compact and neat. They walked into a small entry that connected to the living room.

"Do you think we could get one, too?" she asked, concentrating on closing the door, and placing her purse on a small table.

"One what?"

"A jet." She glanced at him uncertainly. "I want you more than I want anything in this life, Jake. But I want us to have the best chance. I don't want to go stir crazy in Forever."

"So you want to buy a jet?" It was a bit drastic... Okay, it was a lot drastic, but he was willing to consider it.

After all, the woman was giving him a child. She was handing him his dream on a silver platter. The least he could do was meet her halfway.

But a jet?

She nodded.

"If you work for Derek, he'll have you flying in and out all the time." But if she still wanted a jet, he'd get her a jet.

"I turned him down." She chewed on her thumbnail. "He's probably filled the position by now."

Jake chuckled. She was so beautiful when she talked nonsense. "Yeah. Right. Gorgeous, intelligent ambassador types who speak six languages are a dime a dozen in Forever. I'm sure he's filled the job."

"It's a perfect job." Her blue-green eyes glowed with cautious anticipation. "Do you think it's real?"

"Real?"

"I thought you arranged it. I know you wanted me

to stay in Forever. And the job seemed just a little too convenient. And Derek *is* your friend..."

"He's not that good of a friend."

"He lent you his jet."

"His dad's jet. The job is very real."

"The job sounds great."

"*You* look great," said Jake. He pulled her back into his arms. "You feel great. You smell great." He bent to kiss her neck. "You taste out of this world."

"Yeah?" she breathed, arms twining around his neck.

"So, you want to start packing right away?" He kissed her temple. Then he kissed her mouth. His tongue traced the outline of her lips. "Or..."

"Or..." she said, reaching for the buttons on his coat. "Definitely or..."

"Robin," he breathed. He shrugged out of his coat. Then he got rid of her blazer, anxious to remove all of the barriers between them.

He loosened the button on the back of her skirt and slipped a hand down to her bare stomach. It was warm and firm and beautiful. The thought of his child inside her was way past phenomenal.

With his free hand, he cradled the back of her head, pulling her close, touching their foreheads together and letting his ecstasy free-fall.

"This is so right, Jake."

"It's always been right," he whispered through his mounting desire.

"It was then." He brushed her hair back from her

face, gazing at the green iris streaks he'd fallen in love with so many years ago.

"It is now." He tipped his head sideways to kiss her mouth. Once. Then longer. Then longer still.

He lifted her hand between them and ran the pad of his thumb over the little bumps of her wedding ring. "And it will be forever."

COMING SOON...

AN EXCITING
OPPORTUNITY TO SAVE
ON THE PURCHASE OF
HARLEQUIN AND
SILHOUETTE BOOKS!

*DETAILS TO FOLLOW
IN OCTOBER 2001!*

YOU WON'T WANT TO MISS IT!

PHQ401

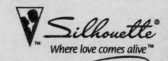

*Harlequin truly does
make any time special. . . .
This year we are celebrating
weddings in style!*

A Walk Down the Aisle
WEDDING CELEBRATION

To help us celebrate, we want you to tell us how wearing the Harlequin wedding gown will make your wedding day special. As the grand prize, Harlequin will offer one lucky bride the chance to **"Walk Down the Aisle"** in the Harlequin wedding gown!

There's more...

For her honeymoon, she and her groom will spend five nights at the **Hyatt Regency Maui.** As part of this five-night honeymoon at the hotel renowned for its romantic attractions, the couple will enjoy a candlelit dinner for two in Swan Court, a sunset sail on the hotel's catamaran, and duet spa treatments.

A HYATT RESORT AND SPA®

Maui • Molokai • Lanai

To enter, please write, in, 250 words or less, how wearing the Harlequin wedding gown will make your wedding day special. The entry will be judged based on its emotionally compelling nature, its originality and creativity, and its sincerity. This contest is open to Canadian and U.S. residents only and to those who are 18 years of age and older. There is no purchase necessary to enter. Void where prohibited. See further contest rules attached. Please send your entry to:

Walk Down the Aisle Contest

In Canada	In U.S.A.
P.O. Box 637	P.O. Box 9076
Fort Erie, Ontario	3010 Walden Ave.
L2A 5X3	Buffalo, NY 14269-9076

You can also enter by visiting www.eHarlequin.com
Win the Harlequin wedding gown and the vacation of a lifetime!
The deadline for entries is October 1, 2001.

HARLEQUIN®
Makes any time special ®

PHWDACONT1

HARLEQUIN WALK DOWN THE AISLE TO MAUI CONTEST 1197
OFFICIAL RULES
NO PURCHASE NECESSARY TO ENTER

1. To enter, follow directions published in the offer to which you are responding. Contest begins April 2, 2001, and ends on October 1, 2001. Method of entry may vary. Mailed entries must be postmarked by October 1, 2001, and received by October 8, 2001.

2. Contest entry may be, at times, presented via the Internet, but will be restricted solely to residents of certain geographic areas that are disclosed on the Web site. To enter via the Internet, if permissible, access the Harlequin Web site (www.eHarlequin.com) and follow the directions displayed online. Online entries must be received by 11:59 p.m. E.S.T. on October 1, 2001.

   In lieu of submitting an entry online, enter by mail by hand-printing (or typing) on an 8½" x 11" plain piece of paper, your name, address (including zip code), Contest number/name and in 250 words or fewer, why winning a Harlequin wedding dress would make your wedding day special. Mail via first-class mail to: Harlequin Walk Down the Aisle Contest 1197, (in the U.S.) P.O. Box 9076, 3010 Walden Avenue, Buffalo, NY 14269-9076, (in Canada) P.O. Box 637, Fort Erie, Ontario L2A 5X3, Canada.

   Limit one entry per person, household address and e-mail address. Online and/or mailed entries received from persons residing in geographic areas in which Internet entry is not permissible will be disqualified.

3. Contests will be judged by a panel of members of the Harlequin editorial, marketing and public relations staff based on the following criteria:

   • Originality and Creativity—50%
   • Emotionally Compelling—25%
   • Sincerity—25%

   In the event of a tie, duplicate prizes will be awarded. Decisions of the judges are final.

4. All entries become the property of Torstar Corp. and will not be returned. No responsibility is assumed for lost, late, illegible, incomplete, inaccurate, nondelivered or misdirected mail or misdirected e-mail, for technical, hardware or software failures of any kind, lost or unavailable network connections, or failed, incomplete, garbled or delayed computer transmission or any human error which may occur in the receipt or processing of the entries in this Contest.

5. Contest open only to residents of the U.S. (except Puerto Rico) and Canada, who are 18 years of age or older, and is void wherever prohibited by law; all applicable laws and regulations apply. Any litigation within the Province of Quebec respecting the conduct or organization of a publicity contest may be submitted to the Régie des alcools, des courses et des jeux for a ruling. Any litigation respecting the awarding of a prize may be submitted to the Régie des alcools, des courses et des jeux only for the purpose of helping the parties reach a settlement. Employees and immediate family members of Torstar Corp. and D. L. Blair, Inc., their affiliates, subsidiaries and all other agencies, entities and persons connected with the use, marketing or conduct of this Contest are not eligible to enter. Taxes on prizes are the sole responsibility of winners. Acceptance of any prize offered constitutes permission to use winner's name, photograph or other likeness for the purposes of advertising, trade and promotion on behalf of Torstar Corp., its affiliates and subsidiaries without further compensation to the winner, unless prohibited by law.

6. Winners will be determined no later than November 15, 2001, and will be notified by mail. Winners will be required to sign and return an Affidavit of Eligibility form within 15 days after winner notification. Noncompliance within that time period may result in disqualification and an alternative winner may be selected. Winners of trip must execute a Release of Liability prior to ticketing and must possess required travel documents (e.g. passport, photo ID) where applicable. Trip must be completed by November 2002. No substitution of prize permitted by winner. Torstar Corp. and D. L. Blair, Inc., their parents, affiliates, and subsidiaries are not responsible for errors in printing or electronic presentation of Contest, entries and/or game pieces. In the event of printing or other errors which may result in unintended prize values or duplication of prizes, all affected game pieces or entries shall be null and void. If for any reason the Internet portion of the Contest is not capable of running as planned, including infection by computer virus, bugs, tampering, unauthorized intervention, fraud, technical failures, or any other causes beyond the control of Torstar Corp. which corrupt or affect the administration, secrecy, fairness, integrity or proper conduct of the Contest, Torstar Corp. reserves the right, at its sole discretion, to disqualify any individual who tampers with the entry process and to cancel, terminate, modify or suspend the Contest or the Internet portion thereof. In the event of a dispute regarding an online entry, the entry will be deemed submitted by the authorized holder of the e-mail account submitted at the time of entry. Authorized account holder is defined as the natural person who is assigned to an e-mail address by an Internet access provider, online service provider or other organization that is responsible for arranging e-mail address for the domain associated with the submitted e-mail address. **Purchase or acceptance of a product offer does not improve your chances of winning.**

7. Prizes: (1) Grand Prize—A Harlequin wedding dress (approximate retail value: $3,500) and a 5-night/6-day honeymoon trip to Maui, HI, including round-trip air transportation provided by Maui Visitors Bureau from Los Angeles International Airport (winner is responsible for transportation to and from Los Angeles International Airport) and a Harlequin Romance Package, including hotel accomodations (double occupancy) at the Hyatt Regency Maui Resort and Spa, dinner for (2) two at Swan Court, a sunset sail on Kiele V and a spa treatment for the winner (approximate retail value: $4,000); (5) Five runner-up prizes of a $1000 gift certificate to selected retail outlets to be determined by Sponsor (retail value $1000 ea.). Prizes consist of only those items listed as part of the prize. Limit one prize per person. All prizes are valued in U.S. currency.

8. For a list of winners (available after December 17, 2001) send a self-addressed, stamped envelope to: Harlequin Walk Down the Aisle Contest 1197 Winners, P.O. Box 4200 Blair, NE 68009-4200 or you may access the www.eHarlequin.com Web site through January 15, 2002.

Contest sponsored by Torstar Corp., P.O. Box 9042, Buffalo, NY 14269-9042, U.S.A.

PHWDACONT2

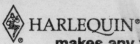